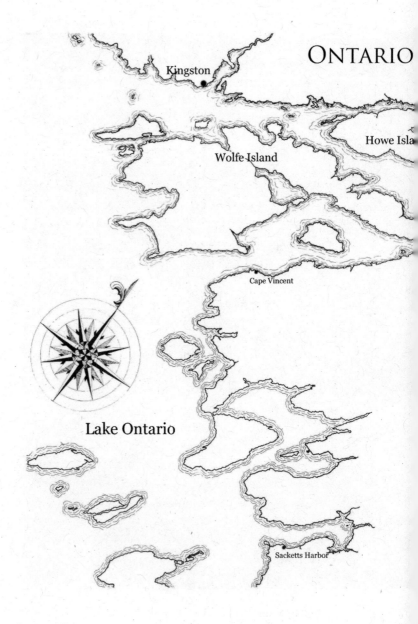

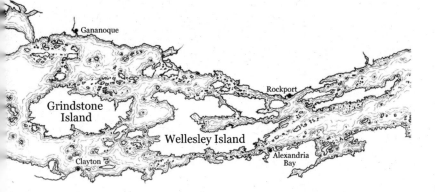

Gananoque

Rockport

Grindstone
Island

Wellesley Island

Clayton

Alexandria
Bay

NEW YORK

● Watertown

5 mi.

Also by Donna Walsh Inglehart

Breaking the Ring

GRINDSTONE

DONNA WALSH INGLEHART

Troubadour Interactive

Epigraph from *Confederate Operations in Canada and New York* by John W. Headley, published by Neale, 1906.

First Edition

Grindstone is a work of fiction. Names, characters, places, and incidents are either the product of the author's imagination or are used fictitiously.

Published in the United States by Troubadour Interactive, LLC

Printed in Canada

Library of Congress – Cataloging-in-Publication Data 2010926095

ISBN 978-1-890642-07-5

Cover photo © Ian Coristine   1000 Islands Photo Art
www.1000islandsphotoart.com

Cover and book design by Dave O'Malley   Aerographics Creative Services
www.aerographics.on.ca

Map: Courtesy of Marilyn & Alan Hutchinson Corbin's River Heritage
www.corbinsriverheritage.com

Production and design: Caitlin Inglehart

Printing: Gilmore Printing Services, Inc. www.gilmoreprinting.com

Troubadour Interactive, LLC   P.O. Box 256   Hebron, Maine 04238
www.troubadourinteractive.com

For David, Caitlin, & Dana Inglehart

and in memory of my mother,

Sybil Carlson Walsh

There is little consolation in relating the particulars of the hostile operations along the northern borders of the United States, by Confederate soldiers from Canada, who were assigned to this service by the authorities of the Confederate States in 1864.

And yet the authentic narrative of this desperate warfare...may serve as a lesson and a guide to the present and future generations of our reunited country in determining the price of peace and the pretexts for war.

Confederate Operations in Canada and New York
John W. Headley, 1906

P R O L O G U E

EVERY MORNING BUT SUNDAY I watched them depart, Finn and my father heading off to the schoolhouse, my long-legged brother matching strides with our da. By then my father had lost all of his faith and much of his hope; mostly charity remained as he taught without pay the few lads left to learn. And discipline, his belief that routine gives shape and therefore meaning to the day. For logic, one studied Latin, for truth, the Greeks. It irked me that they should leave me behind, for I thought myself twice as clever as my twin. So when Finn returned at tea, I made much of the time spent with my mother, of our mornings exploring the shore in search of kelpies and mussels, climbing up to the faerie ring that overlooked Tawny Bay.

During the day the ring was safe enough, for the faeries only did their mischief at night. We sat in the sun high above the sea, watching the shadows of the clouds on the hillside, my mother's hand on my own as she helped me to shape my letters. Her hands were rough, for as a girl she'd mended the fishing nets alongside her mother. Her years as a wife had not softened them, although she had married the Scottish landlord's son and could have had help. Nor had they softened her temper, as sharp and quick as her laughter.

When I open the door to memory, I hear her voice reciting the old verses, the ones that proclaim our glory days. It was she who chose our names for their power and wisdom: *Fionn*, the great hero of Irish myth, *Aine*, Queen of the Faeries. My father had indulged his pretty wife in this fancy, but the names soon became a source of pain for him for their

1

terrible irony.

An Gorta Mor, The Great Hunger: a million dead, millions more leaving Ireland on ships rife with typhus and cholera. The English, who had starved us, observed that with so many departed, a man could now have a decent portion of land to support his children. "They have no shame, no decency! We are *not* 'better off!'" My father shook the cottage with his anger. He tore through the newsprint until he found the quotation. "Here, read what the German, Marx, has written: 'After being starved into ruin, the Irish are good only for whoring and begging.'" By then the rift between my father and his own family was complete, his father and mother returned to Scotland, the plantation manor left in the hands of the British overseer.

I understood even as a child that my mother filled my days with heroes and faeries to replace the faith my father had lost. She did not know how many hours Finn and I spent exploring the empty cottages that had once held our playmates. Some had been buried near the kitchen gardens because the church yards were overcrowded, their unsanctified graves piled high with stones to keep animals away.

Like so many others, Father began to look to America for salvation. He was convinced of its bounty: there a man could raise his children to believe in the possibility of dignity, of dreams. Our mother was adamant that we remain in Ireland. Although the days of the coffin ships had passed, the journey was still dangerous, the cities brutal. Those who survived arrived desperate and ill, welcomed only by kin. She would not leave her home for such an uncertain future.

In the end, it was no dream of bounty that carried us to America. As Finn grew older, Father came to recognize in his son his own idealism, corroded with a hatred of everything English. It seemed inevitable that were he to remain in Ireland, Finn would join one of the secret brotherhoods, ending up imprisoned or dead. So our father cast our fates to the winds that would carry us across the Atlantic. Ten weeks, the voyage took, and as fate would have it, Finn and I were left to survive on our own. Our mother died before we stepped aboard the *Marguerite,* our father, in Kingston, Ontario, in the aftermath of the terrible journey.

I was twenty when this story begins, living in the state of New York on a rough granite island named Grindstone, just below the headwaters of the St. Lawrence River. By then Finn had gone for a soldier and I was alone. In the atlas Grindstone looked like a country unto itself, surrounded by a hundred lesser islands, inhabited, I was certain, with bears and wild men. When I came to that place, it was October, and the trees were red and gold. Then November came, with its somber skies, December, when all living things seemed to abandon the land, and the river boomed and cracked as it seized up in ice. Then everything froze altogether, and the sky and the water became still.

New to that country, caught up in my own survival, I did not understand the scope or nature of the War of the Rebellion, only that it was not ours, my brother's and mine, to fight. I could not have imagined that the war would come to the very shores of Grindstone, with such treachery and brutality that I still wake at night with a pounding heart.

But when I open the door to memory, I am leaning against the warm stones of the faerie ring, a piece of slate in my lap. Sun on my face, breeze from the sea on a May morning in Kilcar, County Donegal. My mother's hand on my own as she helps me to shape my letters. In the deliberate turning of chalk, my name appears: *Anya O'Neill MacGregor*. In the fusion of chalk and slate, I shape words, and with words, meaning.

"If it's not written," my mother told me, "it won't stand. Do not leave it to others. Only you will be able to tell your own story."

CHAPTER 1

Clayton, New York
November 1864

DAWN BROKE as *The Islander* set forth from Grindstone, illuminating the mist that hung heavy on the channel. Inside the cabin the pilot cursed to himself. He would have to feel his way to the mainland, his compass of little use in the eddying currents. No help at all in avoiding the steamers from Toronto or the acre-wide timber rafts that swept downstream. Nothing to do but to forge ahead. An act of faith, it was, and all for the sake of three passengers.

One of them, the Irish girl, was making her way toward the pilothouse, gripping the railing as if they were crossing the north Atlantic. She'd been hired to replace the island schoolmaster, Bill Monson. Poor sod, took a shot in the gut at Petersburg. At first the islanders thought that they'd made a bad bargain: "A. O. MacGregor" turned out to be a woman and Irish, not Scottish, as her surname had led them to believe. Then she had stepped off the ferry with her sorry carpetbag and neatly mended gown, looking barely older than her pupils, and they decided to make the best of it.

"Don't worry, miss," he called out. "We'll get through it."

Anya watched the pilot peering at his instruments, muttering to himself. She had little confidence in the old man: she had smelled whisky on his breath when she'd climbed aboard. Likely as not they'd end up at the bottom, like the barge that hit a shoal a few weeks earlier, three people drowned. She leaned over the railing but could see nothing in the swirling mist. It was as if they had already entered the afterworld.

Then she heard the clamor of activity on the waterfront, and Clayton emerged from the fog, a jumble of rough buildings lining the shore. Barges and work boats crowded the town landing, where men loaded wagons lined up along the quay. Steering his way among the larger vessels, the pilot eased the ferry to its assigned pier and shut down the engine. As the ferry coasted up to its berth, a lad reaching for the line slipped and fell into the river. He flailed his arms, kicking at the skim ice. It took several minutes to haul him out with a grapple hook, and then he was laid out on the pier, bystanders covering him with their coats. By then the boy had turned stiff as a corpse, only his eyes showing any life. Anya pressed forward in the crowd, searching his face. She didn't recognize the lad. After a moment he began to stir, and she moved along, pulling her cloak around her.

Anya had already survived two months on Grindstone and believed that surely it was the coldest place on earth. Only November, and already she fed the fire all night to keep from freezing, pulling her mattress as close to the hearth as was safe. Still, by morning the water bucket had iced over and hoarfrost coated the walls. The great flocks of geese had departed weeks ago.

Hiking through the village, Anya regretted again her move to the island. Clayton bristled with the rough energy of expansion: since October three stone buildings had been built on James Street, more substantial than the wood-framed cottages that lined the harbor. A zig-zag of planks stretched the length of Water Street, the road itself a muddy morass, churned up with the heavy loads of timber hauled from the barges. Men and boys walked alongside the draft horses, clucking, yanking on their bridles. Despite the cold, Anya lingered a bit, caught by the window displays, sorely tempted to step inside.

She was still unused to America's abundance. Even with the war shortages, the shelves were laden with food—gleaming jars of preserved fruits, fine-milled bread, slabs of bacon. Then she noticed the sign, stenciled in neat letters:

HELP WANTED: NO IRISH NEED APPLY

Six months earlier, Anya would have yanked down the sign, but she had learned the hard way that there was no point. The notices were everywhere, some in much cruder language. "A mick is a nigger turned inside out," someone briskly explained. "I'd hire a black man over a bogger any day."

The path to Brady's Mercantile cut down by the shipbuilders' wharves, where shanties and taverns elbowed for space along the harbor. The air was thick with wood-smoke and the smell of cooking: fried fish and boiled winter vegetables. Here the newcomers camped, the Irish and Italians and free blacks, living on top of one another, competing for whatever work they could find. Sometimes the taverns were disorderly during the day, men spilling out onto the lane drunken and rowdy. A few desperate women lingered about the muddy lanes hawking themselves. The constable stayed away, letting the newcomers settle their differences.

As she rounded the corner, Anya saw that a crowd had gathered in front of the shop. She moved to the edge of the group, straining to hear as a man on the porch called out the names on the casualty list, Lonsway, McArdle, Birch...six from Clayton alone. Each name came as a blow to someone in the crowd, and Anya looked away, frightened, as this mother, that father, received the news. When the crowd finally dispersed, Anya leafed through the back pages, searching for her twin brother's name.

Last April, Anya had watched Finn board the train at Sackets Harbor with the other lads who had joined the 94th Infantry Regiment. She had been angry with him, and their parting words had been sharp. As the line had begun to move, she had not been able to distinguish him from the others. "Oh, Finn," she had whispered. And as if he had heard her, he turned and waved to her, pulling a merry face. Then he was gone.

In the low-ceilinged store, the air was thick with tobacco and wood smoke. Men jostled for space around the stove, stepping over the enormous, filthy dog that sprawled in front of it. Anya stood by the wall, listening for news of the 94th. Try as she might, she could make little sense of their conversation, a jumble of names and places, more battles, more death. It would never be over. She looked up at the framed illustration of Abraham Lincoln. For the hundredth time she cursed the man she held responsible for the war and all of the pain it had wrought.

Seamus Brady, a burly, red-haired Dubliner, emerged from the back room and saw the lass standing by the counter, fidgeting with impatience. She stopped in almost every week to post something or ask for her mail, rarely spending money on anything else. She had first appeared in his shop a few months earlier, a stringy bit, wary as a feral cat. He'd thought she'd meant to steal something, but she'd only been looking for work. A dozen questions, she'd had; she could read and write, she could manage his accounts. Her Donegal accent had become stronger as she became more animated, and he had listened with pleasure to its cadence; the Donegal clans were known for their independence, even in Dublin. The lass passed herself as married, but he doubted this to be the case, too many patches in her story. Likely she lied to protect herself: a married woman on her own was safer than a maid. He had admired her mettle and was sorry to turn her away. He'd since heard that she had managed to secure a decent position, schoolmistress on that God-forsaken island. The pay was next to nothing, but it was better than the laundries or whoring – he hated to see the newcomers fall so low.

"*Dia dhuit*, Mrs. MacGregor!" Good day.

"*Dia dhuit*," she said. Brady made her nervous. She knew he ran that part of town with a hard hand.

"How's life on Grindstone?" He laughed, folding his arms. "The islanders are a queer folk, aren't they? Keep to themselves." When she didn't respond, he pulled a wooden crate from under the counter and leafed through the contents. Finally he shook his head. "Sorry, m'am. Nothing since the last bit."

"Are you certain?" She looked if she would grab the lot and search for herself.

"Nothing today, Mrs. MacGregor," he said. "I'm truly sorry."

"It's been such a long time since I've heard anything." She stopped to compose herself. "I've written so many letters. Do you think they've gotten through?"

The lass was barely holding herself together. "Some will," he said. "And look here. The newspaper says that Sherman has taken Atlanta. It won't be long now. The general's broken the spine of the South."

To Anya it was only more war talk. She opened her satchel and pulled out a twine-bound bundle, setting it on the counter. "It's for Christmas." She felt near to tears. Surely there would be a truce for Christmas Day?

He looked at the address, nodded briskly, then placed the package in a sack by his feet. "All right, then. He reached over to pat her hand then stopped himself. She would not welcome his touch. "He'll find his way back to you, don't worry yourself." His face grew solemn. "And you must have faith, Mrs. MacGregor. I'll say a prayer."

She looked at him then, her dark eyes angry. "As you wish," she said. "I don't pray anymore."

Neither did he. Not a breath of a prayer since he lost his youngest lad at Gettysburg. But he didn't like seeing the lass in such a state. "Mrs. MacGregor," he said finally.

She was fussing with her purse. "I'd like a packet of tea and a half-pound of flour. And the postage. How much?"

As he wrapped up her trifling purchases, Brady added some bread and a slab of cheese, and a few worn copies of *The Reformer*. He watched as she considered his offerings, as if she were a wild thing he were trying to tame.

After a moment, she slipped the bundles into her bag. "Thank you," she murmured, then made her way through the crowded store.

As she stepped into the street, Anya cursed herself. She was next to an idiot to accept anything from Seamus Brady. He was a bully and an instigator, the very sort her father had warned Finn against; she had heard a rumor that he had a hand in the Fenian Brotherhood. But she knew what Finn would say: her father wasn't here to protect her, was he then? At least she would eat that night.

Anya could hardly bear the thought of returning to Grindstone, and so she spent the rest of the day exploring the village, wandering in and out of the shops and down by the shipyards. She stopped to listen to a motley group of musicians huddled around a fire, caught by the sounds of home. Then she went into St. Mary's Church to warm herself, retreating when she saw the parish priest getting ready to hear confessions.

The sun was already low in the sky as she hurried to the landing. The boat was packed with sundry goods, wire bales, grain, lamp oil. Every seat was taken, and for once Anya welcomed the crowd, for in its density she could find shelter from the wind. As the ferry pulled away from the dock, the current caught and held it until the engine gained speed, pushing them upriver.

Anya pulled her cloak around herself, turning away from the wind. Without news from her brother, she was returning to the island sorely disappointed. Still, the village had provided momentary refuge from the bleakness of island life. She would come more often, the fare wasn't that dear. And with the number of hotels being built, she might even find work. Anya turned and looked back at the mainland. The docks were almost empty, most of the smaller boats hauled ashore that very afternoon. She could see the masts of the schooners that filled French Creek Bay, where they had been secured for winter. A few bonfires blazed down by the wharves, and she imagined men and women huddled close to the flames, the only source of heat through the long winter's night.

When the ferry docked at Aunt Jane's Bay, the pilot said, "The ice is setting up pretty good. Likely this is the last trip for awhile."

"What?" Anya turned to him, stricken. "But what will we do?"

"Wait," said the old man. "Wait it out. End of January, the ice'll be thick enough to walk to Clayton." He laughed. Small comfort there. He wished his passengers well, then lit the running lanterns and turned the boat back to the mainland. The engine made a chuffing sound, sending up gouts of steam into the thin evening light. The group watched in silence, forlorn, Anya thought, as refugees adrift on a new continent.

CHAPTER 2

City of New York

EVEN IN NOVEMBER, the streets of New York were filthy, crowded with livestock, immigrants, and soldiers milling about in the mire. On every corner hung an effigy of Lincoln as grotesque and obscene as any in the South. **THE ILLINOIS APE**, the signs read. At night the strawmen were torched by carousing, angry mobs, illuminating the city. How had Lincoln been re-elected?

He stood in the shadows, watching the entry to the tavern. The place was crowded, and in his tradesman's clothes, he would pass unnoticed. He now called himself Douglas, Jonathon Douglas; he would use this name for as long as it suited his purpose. He stood near the bar, as if waiting to order a whisky. A playbill caught his attention:

Winter Garden Theatre · November 25, 1864

THE WORLD-FAMOUS BOOTH BROTHERS
Edwin, Junius Brutus, & John Wilkes Booth
On Stage Together FOR THE FIRST TIME

in

William Shakespeare's Masterpiece

JULIUS CAESAR

PRODUCTION TO BENEFIT CENTRAL PARK'S BRONZE OF SHAKESPEARE

John Booth looked handsome in his theatrical portrait, although the likeness could not convey the man's vitality, the magnetism that drew men and women to him wherever he traveled. For that very reason, Booth did not make a good spy. He burned with Confederate fervor and had proven in the past to be unstable. Better that he burn on stage in Shakespeare's tragedy. Which role would he assume, tyrant or assassin?

Douglas had seen Booth just a month earlier in Toronto, where they had met with Jacob Thompson, John Headley, and the Kennedy brothers to finalize the plans to overthrow the Union election. They had set their sights on New York, where McDonald had already bribed military and local officials. The mayor was in their pocket.

Then, just three days before the election, the conspiracy was uncovered. Douglas could still see Katie McDonald's stricken face as she signaled them from an upstairs window. Her father had been betrayed, and the house in Brooklyn was packed with Union detectives, upending beds and dumping bookshelves and wardrobes, searching for evidence of the conspiracy. McDonald was hauled off to prison and within a day Union troops were pulled from the front to stand guard by the voting polls and warehouses.

It was a hard blow, but they were men already hardened by battle. And now Sherman had waged a firestorm through Georgia, destroying everything in his path. "We are not only fighting hostile armies," Sherman had said, "but a hostile people, and must make old and young, rich and poor, feel the hard hand of war. I can make Georgia howl."

The election plot having failed, the conspirators would now make New York howl. Though their numbers were few, they had the most powerful weapon of all: terror.

Douglas pulled out his watch. Half past seven. He slung his satchel over his shoulder and left the tavern. A few Union soldiers loitered about on the corner. War-weary, the men gazed at P.T Barnum's poster:

TONIGHT! At the AMERICAN MUSEUM THREE MAMMOTH FAT GIRLS, WEIGHING ONE TON! THREE GIANTS, TWO DWARFS, 17 POUNDS EACH!!!

The place would be packed, of course, with at least two thousand spectators. Rob Kennedy said he would handle that one: he liked a good joke.

Two days earlier Douglas had gone with John Headley to the chemist in Brooklyn. The young veterans had been assigned by Thompson to pick up the incendiary, three dozen bottles of Greek fire, enough to torch nineteen hotels and several warehouses in the city. Headley had stood watch outside the shop while Douglas paid the old man with gold coins, packing the vials carefully into an old carpetbag. "Very powerful--used by the Phoenicians and the Romans," the chemist told them. Douglas had later divided the vials among the eight conspirators, giving them their instructions.

Douglas now headed down Broadway, pulling his cap over his dark hair. Headley emerged from a doorway and fell in step beside him. They walked for a few blocks in silence, Headley gesturing to the confusion of carriages and wagons that clogged the streets. It was obvious that the fire wagons would never get through, that the buildings would burn to the ground. People would be trapped in the staircases and in the alleyways. City blocks would turn to rubble as if they'd been bombarded.

Finally Headley spoke. "I'm worried about Rob Kennedy."

"Drunk?"

"No. He's feverish, excited. I told his brother to keep an eye on him."

The city's church bells began to chime. Eight o'clock.

"All right then," said Headley. "For the Southland."

"For the Southland."

Douglas watched John Headley slip away into the crowd. Headley would take the Astor and the Metropolitan. He himself would head to the Belmont, where he had registered under the name "John School," the sleepy clerk barely noting his signature.

The plans were simple, identical: in the rented rooms, pull the mattresses off the beds and stack on top of them light furniture and any ready debris. Break the wax seals on the vials and pour the contents onto the pile, then light the fuses. The fuses were slow-burning and would give them time to escape.

When the hotel clerks investigated the smoke, they would see the flames and attempt to douse the mattresses with water. At that moment the rooms would explode. That was the beauty of Greek fire, its mortal simplicity: it was ignited by water. Fire would rage through the hotels, the barges, the granaries. By nine o'clock, the entire city would be torched. They would bring New York to its knees, then onto Philadelphia, Buffalo, Detroit. And in the end, the Union.

CHAPTER 3

AS THE FERRY DEPARTED, Emmet Dodge pulled up to the landing with his hay wagon to carry the passengers up the long hill to the island road. There were so many aboard that his massive draft horses strained on the rise, their hooves slipping on the ice, and the younger passengers climbed down to lighten the load.

One of Anya's pupils hiked the frozen ground beside her, too shy to speak. Ten years old, tall for his age, Erik Karlson still had trouble with his letters. Once in frustration, Anya put her hand on his in order to guide him, but he jerked it away as if she had scalded him. Erik knew that his mother blamed the new teacher for his failure to learn. It was because she was Irish, she'd said; his brother had learned to read and write well enough from the previous schoolmaster. And indeed, from the front, Nils had written letters to his family in his neat script. Now both his brother and his schoolmaster were dead, turning to dust in a strange land. What difference did it make if he learned how to write?

They boarded again at the center road. This part of the island had been gentled, the forest timbered, fields cultivated with wheat and barley, but in November Anya thought the place looked barren as a peat bog. As they headed north, Erik's farm finally appeared, a small tidy house with a large barn. At the sound of the hooves a dog ran up the lane, Erik's younger brother racing behind it, shouting halloos. Anya imagined preparations for supper well underway, lamps lit, a savory stew bubbling on the stove, windows fogged with steam. Erik's mother would be setting plates on the table, his father mending tack by the fire.

When Erik climbed down, Anya felt such a weight on her heart that she could hardly say goodbye.

Anya lived on the outermost reach of the island, so she was last to disembark. The driver scrutinized the shadowed footpath that led to her cabin. "Mrs. MacGregor, this place is too rough for a young lady such as yourself." He climbed down, then helped Anya to the ground. "Some's been complaining about missing things. You shouldn't be alone out here. It's not right."

Anya was all too aware of the isolation of her cabin. "Truly, Mr. Dodge, I'm not worried. I'm safe."

He looked again at the path and shook his head. "Keep the door bolted. And don't leave women's things about, you know, hanging on the line. Should look like a trapper camp." His voice was filled with frustration. "See here, Mrs. MacGregor, why don't you move in with us? We've got the room."

She thought about the Dodge farm, with its muddy yard and creamery, bursting at the seams with cows and grandchildren, cats and chickens forever underfoot. Four grown daughters, his only son Teddy run off to sea. Marla, his wife, who stopped speaking one day, no one knew why.

"I appreciate your offer, Mr. Dodge, surely I do. My cabin is so near the school, no one would think to bother me."

"What you need is a dog."

"No dogs." Anya made herself smile. "I wouldn't know what to do with one!" When she was a child, the dogs that had escaped being eaten traveled in packs like wolves, foraging in the unmarked graves.

Mr. Dodge waited until Anya crossed the narrow bridge before turning the wagon homeward. As the shadows lengthened, Anya took consolation in the friendly clatter of hooves as his horses made their way down the lane. By the time she reached the cabin, however, the light had gone out of the day. Only the chimney top caught a thin patch of sun. A raven lit on a branch above her, its call harsh and insistent. No sign of the small grey cat she'd been trying to tame, leaving bits of food by the woodshed. The place felt as empty as it had when she'd first arrived.

The cabin wasn't much larger than a shed, just one room with three small windows and a shallow fireplace. When Anya opened the door, she saw that the hearth had gone cold, so she set the kindling. She had quickly learned how to make a decent wood fire. While not as hot or steady as peat, it could liven the place and provide entertainment in its way. A dangerous replacement for human company, that she knew. One could easily become morbid or fanciful when so much alone, sitting before a fire. She'd start listening for the *pookah*, the demon horse with the yellow eyes, who would call for her outside her cabin. Or worse, the *dullahan*, carrying his own glowing head as he rode by. The old tales of cunning and romance could gain too much power.

Her cabin would soon fill with shadows; the long night stretched ahead. As Anya stoked the fire she thought about Mr. Dodge's offer. Perhaps he was right. She knew that the islanders worried about her living alone, for they understood how dangerous the winters of Grindstone could be. From the outset they had urged Anya to board with a family with an extra room; with so many sons gone off to war, there were several possibilities. When she refused, the women brought fruit and vegetables from their own winter stores, curtains and quilts and rag rugs to fend off the cold. Their husbands, the ones too old to fight, had hauled and stacked several loads of firewood – a mountain of wood – enough to worry her about the severity of the winter. They'd been kind to her, despite their initial disappointment. Even so, she remained suspicious of them, for she knew what some had said behind her back.

While the fire took hold, Anya broke off a bit of the cheese and ate it standing before the hearth. Then she stepped onto the porch. The sky was obliterated by clouds; she wondered if it would snow by morning. She called a few times for the cat and thought she saw movement in the shadows, so she left some crumbs by the door. Then she hauled in another load of chestnut to stock the wood box, lighting the lamp by the bed. She retrieved the soapstone bed warmer from the hearth and slipped it under the covers, for the mattress was cold as a grave.

Anya pulled the newspapers and bread from her satchel and sat cross-legged on the rug in front of the fire. Despite her resentment, Anya was grateful to Brady for the papers. They meant as much to her as the food. She read every word, the news items, the advertisements, the obituaries. She was hungry for words, everything held something of interest for her. Of particular curiosity was the story on the front page:

THE FRONTIER
EXCITEMENT AT OGDENSBURG
Appearance of Armed Men on the St. Lawrence
INTENTIONS OF THE NEFARIOUS SCOUNDRELS
Important Information from the State Department
Orders for Peace and Order for the Security of the Elections

Many strangers had flooded the islands; "a raid on the town was feared." Ogdensburg! Although the village was fifty miles downriver, Anya tested the bolt on the door then pulled the curtains snug so that no one could spy on her. Anya picked up the old muzzle-loader that stood by the bed, hefting its weight. It was so balky that it was as likely to explode as to hit anything, but its appearance might fend someone off. Then Anya checked the newspaper date. November 3rd, almost three weeks old. The danger had passed. She resumed her place by the fire and moved on to the next article.

THE SAFETY OF NEW YORK CITY

The following dispatch was received
yesterday by His Honor the Mayor:

Washington, Nov. 3, 1864

This department has received information from
the British Provinces to the effect that there is
a conspiracy on foot to set fire to the principal
cities in the Northern States on the day of the
Presidential election.

W.H. Seward
Secretary of State

Anya would never make sense of the politics of this country. Why would Canadians become involved in the War of the Rebellion? She'd read that the mayor of New York had actually tried to secede from the Union. He didn't give a toss about slavery, he wanted Southern trade for the mills and manufactories.

Anya folded the papers then stood up and stretched. She could no longer see her breath in the air; the small room had quickly warmed. It looked almost cozy in the soft light of the oil lamp, with the covered table and small collection of books. She banked the coals for the night, then packed the food in a tin box. She scrubbed her face and loosened her hair, then slipped into her nightdress. Before she climbed into bed, she reached under the mattress, retrieving a small box wrapped in cloth. Finn had given it to her for their thirteenth birthday, carving it from a hawthorn tree and gluing shells from the cove onto the lid.

Over time the shells had begun to fall off. At first it didn't matter, for there were always shells to be found, but after they had left Ireland Anya suffered a bit with each loss, for she'd lost another piece of home. Anya kept Finn's letters in the box. She had received but three, and the first one was missing a page. The second one was the most painful, but it was the one that she read to strengthen her resolve, to keep from feeling sorry for herself.

She opened it carefully for it was soft as felt, tearing at the folds.

25 April 1864

Dearest Annie,

I have received just four letters from you, although surely it is for certain that you have written more often. The mail is unreliable and so we are grateful for what we get. We share our letters with one another, and your adventures have cheered us all. Annie, you exaggerate! I can hear your voice in your writing - you were always the one to make me laugh, even in Holy Mass when there would be the devil to pay from Father Cleary or worse, our mam. I have described for my comrade soldiers your bright eyes and merry laugh. They have all lined up to marry you when the war is over, even those with wives at home. I did not tell them that you were a rascal, worse than the lads for your deviltry, and that you dance like a colt and sing like a raven.

I am writing to you from the State of Pennsylvania. Our train has stopped in Philadelphia, but we are under guard as if we were criminals, for there is the belief that many of us would run off if we could. We are enlisted soldiers and yet we have not yet been provided with guns for fear that we would turn them on our sergeants.

I don't even dare write to you in Irish - they can't understand it and would accuse me of being a spy.

Some of the lads have barely left their boyhoods behind, and they are frightened half to death. They aren't tough, you see, and sometimes I watch them at night staring at the portraits of their dear ones, very likely their mams, since most are too young for sweethearts. I tell them that such sentiment will keep them soft, and that they were better off to set aside all thoughts of home. It makes me soft just watching them.

Our regiment has been kept somewhat in the dark as to our destination, but I do know that we are being sent to the North of Virginia. From what I've heard, Virginia is a gentler place than New York, with rolling hills and valleys. I imagine it must be a bit like County Clare. We outnumber the opposing army, so we should prevail. I do not underestimate the task, because we will be fighting on Southern Ground, and a man will fight to the end for his Own Land.

Do not worry about me, Sister. Were I to lay down my life in battle, it would be for Ireland and not this place.

I can take care of myself, that you know, so you must not worry when you read news that is hard. It were better that you stay away from the papers altogether. You remember how they broke our da. Stay strong. Remember, Queen Áine, that you are not Alone in this world.

Oíche mhaith dhuit.

Your Brother Finn

Last spring, when Finn wrote that his regiment was being sent to Virginia, Anya reasoned that Virginia was a mild landscape, and at least he'd be warmer there. Then she heard about the battles, that at Antietam the regiments of blacks and Irish were sent first into battle as cannon fodder. Seamus Brady told her that in the Irish Brigade, seven thousand men were cut down to a thousand; one company returned with just seven men. It was a blessing, she thought bitterly, that her father did not live to learn that the new world was no different from the old.

As Anya placed Finn's letter in the box, she knew that nothing would break her except to lose him, and that she would not do. Finn's letters often brought on nightmares, but they also brought him to life, his handwriting as intimate as his breath or the beating of his pulse. Anya believed they restored her to some semblance of herself. She had a brother, she was someone's sister.

Brady said that the war would soon be over. If she did not hear from Finn, she would head south, stopping at every hospital, every prison, traveling to the tip of Florida. She would find him and bring him home. In the atlas she had measured with her hand the distance from New York to Virginia, a span the length of Ireland from Malin's Head to County Cork. The vastness of the country had alarmed her, but when she considered how far it was from the quay at Derry to Aunt Jane's Bay, she knew she could go the distance. No matter what it cost. *Oiche mhaith dhuit*. Good night, dear brother.

CHAPTER 4

THE CONSPIRATORS SET FIRES in nineteen wood-framed hotels in the most congested blocks of the city. Robbie Kennedy hit Barnum's Museum, then they targeted the warehouses packed with combustibles and the kerosene-filled barges jamming the harbor. Finally they made their way to the Five Points to wait, meeting at Pete William's Place. The tavern was crowded, the air unbreathable, and so they went outside, gathering around a torched oil drum. In the yard the night atmosphere was almost as foul; the surrounding tenements were as crowded as rabbit warrens.

Just before nine, the fire bells began to reverberate, one, two, then dozens all at once, all around the city. The men looked at one another, imagining the mayhem, the thousand carriages on Broadway and Fifth jammed together on a Friday night, the impotent fire wagons stalled in the chaos. The horses would be wild with terror. The buildings would fill with smoke, hysterical tenants crowding the stairwells, then the alleyways and streets. When the barrels of kerosene on the barges ignited, the firebomb would illuminate the city. Then the conspirators would slip into the prisons and release and arm their Confederate brethren. The war would shift to a new front. The northern people were unused to battle. They were soft, weak, and would surrender without a fight.

The men sat in the yard, scanning the sky for flames. Soon Rob Kennedy began to drink, talking loudly, laughing. In the jostling crowd he did not draw much attention, even when he began to sing "The Bonnie Blue Flag." A few even joined in; the city was inundated with refugees from the Southern states. His brother Tom watched him closely but did not intervene.

The bells continued to clang but without the urgency they had expected. After awhile they ceased altogether.

"I don't understand," said Headley finally. "Something's gone wrong."

Robert Kennedy stood up and spat in disgust, heading off into the night.

It was not until they read the newspapers the next day that they realized what had happened. The fires had kindled, but one after another, the flaming mattresses had been successfully doused by hotel employees and patrons. They did not combust, there were no explosions. The event had created excitement but little destruction. The newspapers blared the news as if the city of 800,000 had actually been destroyed.

Bombing Plot: One of the most Fiendish and Inhuman Acts Known of Modern Times
New York Times

The Most Diabolical Attempt at Arson and Murder of which there is any Record In our Country

Frank Leslie's Illustrated Newspaper

The hypocrisy was despicable: what did the writers imagine their unleashed hell-hound, General William Sherman, was doing to the citizens of Georgia? With this second failure, the conspirators had been forced to disband, leaving the city, their hopes for defeating the Union destroyed.

A few weeks later, Douglas met with his fellow compatriots in Toronto. They sat in silence around the table where the plans had first been laid out, the room growing dark as evening fell. Then someone stood and lit the lamps and each began to tell his own version of what had happened. All the details had been in place, the locations scouted, the mayor and several prison wardens bought and paid for. One by one, each man had told his piece of the tale: how he had emptied the vials on the mattresses, lit the fuses, and watched until each had taken hold. Something, indeed, had gone wrong. They had been betrayed a second time.

Suspicion had centered, naturally enough, on the chemist. He must have sold them bad goods. He was a counter-spy or, at the very least, a crook.

"I know the man," John Headley had angrily insisted. "He's loyal. I went back to him, showed him one of the empty vials. He smelled it, said it was not what he'd sold us. Said it was nothing more than alcohol."

Then Headley stopped. Something shifted in his expression. He turned to Douglas. "Did you notice anything odd about them? Did you look at all of them?"

"Of course. I saw nothing to make me suspicious." Douglas looked around the table at his friends and comrades, men who had fought alongside him with Lee at Chancellorsville. He shook his head. "I don't know any more than you do. It doesn't make sense."

Thompson raised his hand. "We won't get to the bottom of it this way." His face was filled with despair. They had risked everything and lost. Their last hope of saving the Confederacy was lost.

Douglas left Toronto that afternoon without waiting for the cover of darkness. Most of his clothes still hung in the closet of his hotel room, and a few personal items were scattered on his bureau. They would not notice until the next day that he had actually departed. He left a note for Jacob Thompson at the front desk, alluding to family concerns, and hoped that this would buy him some time. His comrades would find it hard, at first, to question his loyalty, but eventually they would begin to doubt him.

He headed east by stagecoach, making it to Gananoque in less than a week. By then, the St. Lawrence River had frozen solid, and he walked island to island until he found the right place, a small uninhabited island just downriver from Grindstone.

There he discovered a hunter's lay-by, a low-ceilinged log hut dug into an embankment that was all but invisible from the shore. From the rise he could see in all directions—no one would be able to approach him unnoticed. He covered the windows with oil cloth and the dirt floor with deer pelts and cleaned out the small stove. He was well armed and had purchased enough provisions in Gananoque to last for a few weeks. He knew that several villages were strung along the United States mainland; he could visit one, then the next, without establishing an observable pattern. The islands were filled with strangers, in any case, and there was not much risk in venturing forth as long as he stayed away from the hotels. He had spent enough time in the North, moreover, that he could pass easily enough for one of them.

As forbidding as the islands were, he would hide out there for a few months. His comrades would neither forgive nor forget his betrayal, but their first instincts would be to return to their homes in the South to see to their families. When the war ended they would come looking for him, but by then he would be gone from this hard place.

CHAPTER 5

ANYA'S SLEEP HAD BEEN DISTURBED by nightmares, and she awoke so groggy that she could hardly bear to face her young charges. The sun had not yet risen and the cabin was very cold; the fire had long since gone out. She hurriedly dressed, dragging a brush through her tangled hair, looping it into a knot. She knew that if she were just a few minutes late, havoc would reign in the schoolhouse. She had used the switch only once on one of the older lads, and everyone had seen that her heart wasn't in it.

She pulled on her cloak and ran down the frozen path to the schoolhouse. With Christmas just a day away, the children were more boisterous than ever, and despite the cold, it took some effort getting them into the schoolhouse. They milled about the room, stamping their feet to warm them, making ghosts in the air with their breath. Anya shoved more kindling into the balky stove, but smoke billowed into the room before she could shut the door.

"*Imigh sa diabhal!*" she cursed, waving her arms at the smoke. Go to the devil.

"It's colder in here than outside."

"We'll never be warm."

"Why are you late? We thought you weren't coming."

Anya ignored them, letting the chatter swirl around her. Hugging herself against the cold, she hurried to her desk, trying to remember what lessons she'd planned for the day. It didn't really matter—most of her pupils were still working on their alphabets.

"She's not even a proper schoolmaster."

"Yes she is. She's smarter than Master Monson."

"So's my dog. Master Monson's *dead*."

"She is too smarter than your dog," a little one piped up. "Your dog chews its tail."

Anya stood up and brushed the woodchips from her gown. She was not meant for teaching, anyone could see that! She had no patience for the work, no talent; she had no idea how she would get through the rest of the day, not to mention the term. What would Finn think if he saw her? She imagined him standing in the back of the room, snorting in disbelief at the notion of his sister as a schoolmistress. At the very thought she laughed aloud.

Maddie Burns looked at her with interest: her schoolmistress rarely laughed. It was an odd sound, as if that part of her voice were unused. Her brother Michael was like that, since coming back from the war. Just now Anya MacGregor looked like a different person, younger, nicer. Well, it would be terrible living all alone, without a mother or father. You'd have no one to talk to, you'd have to eat by yourself. Was she scared, being alone at night? Even her brother Charlie would be better than no one, and he was only five.

Maddie herself was eleven years old, a wild thing with tangled red hair and torn hems. Her nails were bitten to the quick, mostly out of boredom. She was fearlessness, held in high regard by the other pupils. Anya thought her own mother must have been like that as a girl, racing about the village with her brothers, tormenting the bull that lived on the landlord's estate, stealing eggs from the henhouse, a crime punishable by flogging. No wonder Anya's father had been bewitched by her, relinquishing his own family to marry her.

As the day wore on, her pupils finally settled down, mostly from fatigue and boredom. Well, she was boring herself. She set aside the lesson and gathered the children about her in a circle. She had learned as a lass how to spin a tale from Padraig O'Malley, the village storyteller. He'd lost the sight from one eye and had bad limp, but when he spoke, he drew you in so that before you knew it, you inhabited his imaginary world. You believed every word he said, and why wouldn't you? It was his truth. He had taught her mother, and he told Anya that she too had the vision and that if she practiced she'd one day be better than he. Padraig O'Malley, was he still alive?

Anya began to tell the story of Queen Maeve, the mighty goddess who ruled the ancient lands to the north of *Sligeach*. She didn't mention that Maeve had twenty-two husbands or that her breasts were mountains which could be seen for one hundred miles, only that she had enormous power over men. "She was fierce and strong, as strong as a man, as the most powerful king!"

The children were totally absorbed until they heard the sound of hooves in the schoolyard. Maddie was at once on her feet and at the window.

"Michael's here! My brother!" She ran outside, the rest of the children chasing after her.

Anya added more wood to the stove then stepped onto the porch. Michael Burns remained mounted, speaking to his sister. The children clamored around the young veteran, reverentially patting the bay, as if it, too, had fought for the Union and had not spent its entire life on Grindstone. Anya noticed that Erik Karlson stood aside, watching them. His brother Nils would have been about the same age as Michael had he lived. They must have known each other as lads before they became soldiers. They must have fought alongside Finn.

A month earlier, Maddie had announced with great excitement that her brother had returned, but in the ensuing weeks she had become closemouthed on the subject. Now Anya could see why. Michael would have been handsome, with his strapping frame and red-gold hair, but his expression was closed. He must have taken it hard about his leg; it had been amputated just below the knee. Anya felt uneasy looking at him; was Finn still sound?

She awkwardly approached him; he seemed irritated by the excitement of the children. "Hello, Mr. Burns."

He pulled off his cap. "Ma'm. I didn't mean to ruin the lesson."

"You didn't," she said, trying to cover her embarrassment. It was obvious that she had no control at all over the children. "We were just about to have a recess." When he didn't reply, she continued. "Maddie said you were in the 94th. I wonder if you knew my husband. Finn MacGregor."

"Lots of Irish in the 94th, kept to themselves. Maddie, get your things."

"Why?"

"Just get 'em."

"School's not over," said Anya. "Is something wrong?"

"A blizzard moving in. You can see it upriver. Maddie?"

With that, his sister ran whooping to the schoolhouse.

The others were standing about, shivering. "Get inside," Anya snapped. She did not want to look even more foolish in front of this stern young man. For once they obeyed her. She folded her arms. "Mr. Burns, do you know where the regiment is fighting now?"

Michael looked at her, his expression unreadable. "Still in Petersburg, ma'm." Then he pulled a package from his saddlebag. "Mother sent this for the schooling."

"Tell her thank you."

Then Maddie climbed up on the horse behind him. "Goodbye, Mrs. MacGregor. Happy Christmas!"

"Yes, I almost forgot. Happy Christmas."

Anya watched as Michael let the horse pick its way up the icy path. Had he been like that before the war? He was so like Maddie, in some ways, with those blue eyes, that direct gaze, but it was as if the spark had gone out of him. She looked up at the sky. It was heavy as felt, a few flakes floating softly about her. She knew the calm was deceptive. Until that winter, she had rarely seen snow, and at first she had been enchanted with the way it transformed the drab December landscape. After a few storms, however, Anya understood that it only made life that much harder. Wet skirts and boots froze in a few minutes and took all

GRINDSTONE

night by the fire to dry.

Inside the schoolhouse, the children huddled about the stove. Anya added more wood; on such a day the drafty stove would devour twenty logs. She looked at the children's chapped hands and faces—there was no point in their remaining for the rest of the day. "If you are walking home, you better set out. You mustn't get caught in the storm."

The children cheered, and chattering and bustling about, excitedly gathered their things. She made the younger ones stand still while she wrapped their scarves around their heads and faces. "No mittens? Pull your jumper sleeves over your hands. That will have to do. No dawdling along the way, now go straight home."

"Goodbye, Mrs. MacGregor!" they called in merry voices, racing up the path to the lane. "Happy Christmas!"

It wasn't long before the sledges pulled into the yard for the rest of the pupils. A few of the drivers sent the children back inside with packages, payment for their schooling: a boiled chicken, a basket of fresh eggs.

"Thank you," Anya said, collecting the bundles in her arms. "Goodbye! I shan't see you for a week!" She watched, suddenly morose, as the sledges departed up the lane to the island road. A week on her own now seemed an eternity.

When she entered the schoolhouse, Erik was still packing his satchel. "Erik! You must go home! It's a long hike to your farm. Your mother will be worried."

"Yes, m'am." He ducked his head and bolted out the door.

The stove was now blazing, the iron turning red, and Anya realized that she would have to wait until it cooled before shutting it down for the night. It would not do to burn down the schoolhouse. She closed the damper then hung up her cloak and tucked the food bundles into a basket. She would wrap the eggs in her shawl to keep them from freezing during the walk to her cabin. Then she noticed that Erik had left one of his drawings on her desk, a sketch of a fern frond, detailed as lace. Was it meant for a gift? She picked it up. It was beautiful. How strange that the boy could draw with the accuracy of a botanist yet have such difficulty with his letters.

The lad had been reluctant to leave. Perhaps his mother kept a cold house—some grieved in that way. There would be no tree for the children, no holiday meal. Erik's brother had been killed in Virginia in a place called the Wilderness, like the wasteland of Christ's torment. Anya had read about the battle in a newspaper she'd stolen at the train station just a month after Finn had left. The soldiers had been fighting in a dense thicket, and when the brambles caught fire, those who were wounded could not escape. The fire had raged for three days, and the lads were burned alive, thousands of them, without God's mercy. For three days the woods rang with the sound of men's screams. Finn would have fought alongside Erik's brother; Michael Burns would have been there as well. Seventeen thousand men died in that battle. If Finn had not lost a limb or his life at the Wilderness, he would have been sent on to Cold Harbor, then Spotsylvania. The Wilderness was only the beginning.

Had their father known what was in store for his son, the family would never have left Donegal. They'd read about the war, of course, and knew that immigrants were drafted as soon as they stepped ashore in the United States. Even in Ireland they had heard about the draft riots in the City of New York. So their father had taken a teaching position at Queens College in Kingston, Ontario, where many Irish and Scots had settled, where his family would be safe. But by the time they arrived in Canada, his plans had fallen awry. He had done poorly on the voyage, made worse by the foul quarters in the hold, and when they finally made their way to Kingston, he was too ill to begin a new life. With scant resources, Finn and Anya could do little to help him, and they spent a few desperate weeks in a sorry rooming house on Queen Street trying to nurse him back to health.

They were forced to bury their father in Skeleton Park. At least they had secured for him the dignity of his own space, marked with a wooden cross. At the park thousands of immigrants had been dumped in mass graves, as they had been in the old country during the famine, no better than diseased cattle or sheep. Finn would not allow this indignity for their father. Anya wondered how he'd managed to steal the money to pay the gravedigger, but she didn't ask him.

Kingston was already crowded with Irish immigrants, and only the meanest work could be found. And so Finn had argued that they must leave Canada for America. If he could not find work, he would become a soldier. Starve, enlist or be drafted, those were the choices. He could make $300 just for signing on, enough to set her up until his return.

"No, Finn," she had shouted. "You won't do this for me. Don't think you are doing this for me."

"Annie, don't you see it? We have no choice!" Finn's voice was fierce with grief. "We've nothing left."

At least they'd had each other. Now she had nothing. She had buried the money in a tin canister behind the woodshed. Finn's blood money. She couldn't bear to look at it, she wouldn't use a penny until her brother came back from the war.

Anya dragged the rocker closer to the stove. She opened the door, then sat down to watch the smoldering coals. Where was her twin this Christmas Eve? Finn, with his lanky stride and dark curls, a lad who could not turn down a dare.

One time she had provoked him to climb up to the faerie ring on All Hallow's Eve, the most dangerous night of all. Then she'd had to follow, to keep him safe. No more than eight years old, the two of them taunting each other, screaming as they ran back down the hill to the cottage. They'd been spanked for it, but it had been worth it, they'd both agreed, whispering to each other in the dark after they'd been sent to bed. The *pookah* had chased after them, of that they were certain, Finn had seen its glowing eyes, she'd heard its thundering hooves, heard it calling out their names. "Finnn!" she whispered. *"FINNN!"* and their mother had laughed and their father had shouted at them to be quiet.

Finn told taller tales: he had leapt from the cliffs of Slieve League, the home of Fionn MacCumhaill, his very namesake. Clear to the sea, where the silkies had caught him and carried him off to their underwater kingdom. Sometimes the faeries chased him all the way home, in the form of black hounds or crows. As Finn grew older and his interest turned to the lasses, the hounds became raven-haired witches, enticing him with infinite charm and beauty. In his stories, Finn had always escaped.

CHAPTER 6

ANYA WAS JARRED AWAKE by the sound of the schoolhouse door being unlatched. "Finn?" she whispered.

Coming back to herself, she realized she had dozed off in the rocking chair by the stove. The room was dark and the fire turned to embers—how long had she been asleep? She spoke again, her voice thick. "The children left long ago. They've all gone home." Then, struggling to her feet, "Is someone missing?"

After a moment, a man emerged from the shadows, carrying a rifle. She saw at once that he was a stranger, dressed in the rough clothes of a trapper, a cap pulled over his brow. Suddenly she was afraid. "Please leave," she said sharply. "You have no business here." She picked up the wrought iron poker and moved behind the stove. "What do you want?" she said. She could hear the tremor of fear in her voice. "There's nothing here to steal."

The man set the rifle by the door and pulled off his cap. "I did not mean to frighten you, miss. I did not expect anyone to be here."

"Then why did you enter?"

"I got caught." He smiled, a wide boyish grin. Anya was startled by the transformation. He looked much younger. "I was caught by the storm. I smelled the wood smoke and was only looking for a bit of shelter." He paused. "Forgive my rudeness. I must introduce myself," he said. "My name is Douglas. Reverend Jonathon Douglas."

Anya regarded him without speaking. He did not look like a minister. His dark hair was tangled, his beard, unkempt.

"I work at the prison camp on Wellesley Island. I'm the army chaplain. And you must be the schoolmistress. Miss...?"

"Mrs. MacGregor."

"I am pleased to make your acquaintance, Mrs. MacGregor."

His story did not make sense—he had entered the schoolhouse like a thief. "You have walked all the way here from Wellesley Island?"

"It's not far. The ice is sound."

"But why did you come to Grindstone?"

"I was tracking a deer. No luck." His eyes were intelligent, mild. "I am sorry I frightened you, Mrs. MacGregor, especially on such a wild evening. I did not intend to do so."

She looked at him uncertainly. He sounded educated and he seemed harmless enough. Perhaps his story was true—why would anyone pretend to be a chaplain? She set the poker by the stove. "I was not truly frightened," she said finally. "Not at all."

"Still, I beg your forgiveness. I'll now take my leave."

"Are you going back to Wellesley tonight? The storm looks fierce."

"It's not bad yet." He shoved his hair from his forehead, then pulled on his cap.

The gesture reminded her of Finn. She spoke, her voice hesitant. "You might warm yourself before you go." She gestured shyly toward the fire. "Well, it's not much of one, is it?" She tossed a few logs on top of the embers.

"For just a moment." He pulled off his coat and hung it on a hook by the door. With his back to her, she took the opportunity to scrutinize him more closely. He was not as tall or as thin as her brother, more compactly built. His hair was long, in need of cutting, and he wore an old-fashioned felt weskit like her father's. His boots were worn but well-made, expensive looking. When he turned around, she moved to the table and lit the lamp. She noticed the bundles of food left by her pupils.

"Reverend Douglas, you must be next to starving! I should offer you something to eat before you head off into the wild night." She began to unwrap one of the packages.

"Thank you, ma'm, but I believe I would be eating your wages."

She turned to him. "But it's Christmas Eve."

After a moment, he pulled a chair close to the fire and leaned back with a sigh, stretching out his legs. "Mrs. MacGregor, you are kind."

She cut off a chunk of the corn bread and handed it him.

"Thank you," he said.

She felt awkward eating in front of him, but she was very hungry and sliced a bit for herself, then settled into her rocker.

Douglas was the first to speak. "You seem most conscientious, working so late this evening. How long have you been the schoolmistress?"

"Not so long," she admitted. "They only hired me because they couldn't find anyone else."

"I'm sure that was not the case."

"They'd rather have a man, but there are none left to teach, at least on the island." She paused. "It would go better if I had proper books, but what we have is worse than nothing. Someone donated some awful primers, about children who die when they get into mischief. It's a child's nature to be naughty!"

"I remember them. I never understood what we were meant to learn." He laughed, his dark eyes catching the light of the fire.

Again, she had the sensation that he was much younger than he looked. She was aware of his closeness: he smelled of sweat and wood smoke. "Will you celebrate Christmas at the prison camp?"

"I will. The prisoners are men of faith, even if they are our enemy."

"I think the enemy is one who sent the men into battle."

He looked at her in surprise.

"I do," she said. "Lincoln is the enemy. And the Southern president. Lee."

"Jefferson Davis," he said. "Lee is a general."

"I think war is evil, but the Confederate soldiers must be especially wicked, to kill so many for the sake of slavery."

"They are men," he said wearily. "Just men. Most don't even own slaves. They believed in the Southern cause and couldn't imagine what war would be like. Then they got caught up in it and it was too late." He paused. "I feel sorry for them. The prison camps are…inadequate. You can imagine how hard it is surviving on Wellesley Island in a tent."

"The prisoners live in tents?"

"It's not only the Southerners—the camp has Union soldiers awaiting trial."

"For what?"

"Desertion."

Anya pulled her shawl around her shoulders. In one of her letters, she had urged Finn to run away. *Please, Finn, come home. There are so many soldiers, surely you won't be missed. We can give back the money. I haven't spent it. Let the others fight. It is their war, not ours.* "What will happen to them, those who deserted?"

"They are considered traitors so they will be executed."

"But what if they fought? And only then lost heart? Would the court not take it into consideration?"

He must have caught something in her voice. "Mrs. MacGregor, is your husband a soldier?"

"Aye, he is. He's with the 94th, in Petersburg, Virginia." She paused. She did not want to reveal to him that she lived alone. "I live down the lane with my mother and father. And my brother."

"Your brother is too young to fight?"

"Far too young, he's but a lad."

"He's lucky. The war will end before he's called."

"Yes, he's lucky." After a moment, "Mr. Douglas, where is your family?"

"Philadelphia."

"Finn traveled through Philadelphia. I received a letter from there." She cleared her throat. "Philadelphia must be a grand city," she said dully.

"Not as grand as some. You're Irish, aren't you?

She twisted her mother's wedding ring. "Aye. We made the crossing about ten years ago, when I was but a lass."

"I'm afraid I don't know much about Ireland's history."

She looked at him. "Most don't," she said drily. "They only know about the famine, and they think it was our fault, that we are so stupid we only know how to grow potatoes." Her voice became bitter. "But *everything* belonged to the English, everything but the cursed potatoes. They left us nothing." She stopped, embarrassed by her outburst.

After a moment he spoke, his voice kind. "Then tell me about your home. Please. So I am less ignorant."

Anya threw a few sticks of wood into the stove then settled back into her chair. "Where to begin? A village by the sea, like any other. Boats in the harbor, a string of whitewashed cottages along the lane." She cleared her throat. "My gran mending the nets." She flexed her fingers. "So hard on her hands. The hillsides wild with fuchsia in the spring." She looked at him. "Bits and pieces, that's how I remember it, not the whole cloth. I worry that I shall no longer be able to see it."

"Do you think you'll ever go back?"

"There's nothing for us there. Ireland won't be right for a hundred years. When the Irish get stronger they'll fight the English, and that war won't ever end. The anger is so deep it is bottomless. That was why my father wanted us to leave."

"I suppose that's how it will be in the South," he said. "After the war."

"Did you ever travel there before the war?"

"Many times. It was beautiful."

"Did you see slaves?"

"I did."

"I've only read about it, and the battles and all. It seems a cursed place. I try to imagine Finn wandering about that unfamiliar land, and I think it must be so strange for him, so different from what he knows."

He was silent for awhile. "Yes, it would be strange. One longs for home; it's the oldest story. Odysseus's heart was all but broken for longing."

She looked at him in surprise. Her father had loved Homer, had read *The Iliad* and *The Odyssey* aloud after supper, sitting before the peat fire, his family around him. She had never tired of the story, the sound of her father's voice as he assumed the roles of the different characters.

Then he stood and set the chair by the table. "Mrs. MacGregor, your father will be on his way; he will want you home on Christmas Eve. And he might be upset to find you sharing your stove and your gifts with a strange man!" He smiled again, pulling on his coat and cap. "Happy Christmas, Mrs. MacGregor. I won't forget your kindness. May God bless you."

He grabbed his rifle and stepped out into the swirling snow.

CHAPTER 7

HE WATCHED FROM THE WOODS as she locked the school-house door. She pocketed the key then paused for a moment, obviously reluctant to enter the storm. Then she pulled her cape about herself and hurried up the forest path, making her way by lantern through the drifting snow. She was obviously heading to the cabin he'd discovered on the rise just north of the schoolhouse. As he had suspected, there was no family, no farm down the lane. She lived alone.

It was snowing hard now, and he considered his options. Maple was no more than a mile's hike across the ice, but in the storm he could easily miss the island. Patches of the river had not yet frozen, and in the dark he would not see the open water until it was too late. After just a month on the island, he could no longer trust his instincts. How had he made such a careless mistake? When he had come upon the darkened schoolhouse, he had seen smoke billowing from the stove pipe. Why had he assumed no one was there? Worse, he had frightened the woman, raising her suspicions. If she were questioned, she would be able to identify a sketch of him. Had he actually pulled off his clumsy deception? He recalled her shy smile. Yes, she had believed him, but he could afford no more blunders.

The wind had picked up, and he decided it would be worse than foolhardy to try to make it to his camp. Hands shaking with cold, he picked the lock of the schoolhouse door. The room was still warm. He threw more logs into the stove, pulled of his boots, then spread his long coat on the floor and settled in for the night. He would sleep better than he had in weeks.

Even if their encounter had been a mistake, he had to admit that he had enjoyed talking with the Irish woman. It had been a long time since he'd spoken with anyone at all. She was as shy and awkward as a servant, but engaging in her way. How difficult it must be for her, living alone in this hard place, her husband off to war. He pulled a volume from the shelf and looked at the cover. He hadn't seen such a primer since his childhood. He flipped through the pages then set it back on the shelf. She was right, the tales were tedious. No child should be made to read such rubbish.

He thought about the library in the house in Richmond, shelves to the ceiling filled with beautifully bound books, worn, well-read. How were they faring, his mother and sister, with no one to protect them? The schoolmistress looked to be the same age as his sister. Sara, who had wept like a child when their mother made her pack away her silk and beribboned gowns, unseemly in a time of war.

The storm was worse than Anya had expected, gathering strength, howling about her cabin, rattling the windows. She hauled in an extra load of wood, hoping she had enough for the duration. She had plenty of food and water, but if the fire went out, she would die.

As she unpacked her satchel, Anya wondered if Jonathon Douglas had reached his destination. In such a storm he might easily have lost his way to Wellesley Island. She should have offered to let him stay the night in the schoolhouse. He'd seemed harmless enough, even though he had given her a bad fright. Well, it was too late for that. He was a soldier and surely could find his way on his own. Still, she hated to think of him struggling home on such a bitter night.

Anya set the packages on the table. There were several, more than

she had expected, especially at a time of year when people had begun
to dig into their winter storage. Potatoes, onions, turnips, the cornbread from Mrs. Daltry. Cora Burns had packed a jar of preserved fruit,
pressed cheese, and a small cake. Included was a note written in a girlish
hand:

Thank you for teaching Maddie to read

CB

The gift was generous, especially given the family's hard circumstances—Mr. Burns was known to be something of a failure as a farmer.
Anya was glad that she had thought to share her food with Jonathon
Douglas. He had seemed a decent man, comforting the soldiers, poor
men, so far from home at Christmas. In November she had sent Finn a
letter along with a twist of tobacco and some candy. She had knit him
a muffler and a pair of socks from a shawl she had unraveled, knotty
tangled things that would likely give him blisters. But they still carried
the smell of peat from their cottage, and she hoped the scent, in itself,
would be a comfort.

Reverend Douglas must have a house on the island; it seemed unlikely that he would share a tent with the prisoners. She wondered if he
lived alone. He had said nothing of a wife or child, but then, she had
done all the talking. She had chattered like a magpie! It was difficult
to guess his age, for those who had gone for soldiers looked older than
their years. Michael Burns could pass for thirty, but she doubted he was
older than she. As Anya settled before the fire she wished she had asked
Jonathon Douglas more questions. It was so hard to find out anything
about the soldiers and what their lives were like on the front. Those who
had fought seemed unwilling to speak of it. She wished he had been able
to stay a bit longer, for it had been pleasant talking with him. She spent
her days with children and although they sometimes made her laugh,
pulling her from her gloom, they were not enough.

The wind was so strong that it was drawing the heat up the chimney, and so she closed the damper as much as she dared and threw a few more logs onto the fire. She found herself thinking of Aiden McLaughlin, who had caught her heart when she was fifteen. Aiden, with his blue eyes and wild ways, her brother's best friend. She'd been jealous of him for taking her brother away from her, and then she herself had fallen hard. She thought of Aiden every waking minute and could hardly breathe for wanting him. Then she had kissed him and made him her own, and it was Finn who was jealous, for he'd lost a friend as well as a sister, at least for awhile.

Aiden was one of the lads who joined the secret brotherhood. He would stop at their cottage after supper, tipping his cap to her parents, gesturing to Finn to step outside. She would listen at the window to their whispered, angry conversations. Sometimes Finn would go off with Aiden, and when he returned to the cottage, he avoided their father, heading directly to bed. As hard as she pressed him, Finn refused to tell her what was going on, and it created a rift between them. Finally Aiden left the village, for it was no longer safe for him, and he had already brought trouble onto his family. They later heard that he had gone to New Zealand.

Aiden once told her she was the most beautiful lass in the village, in all of Ireland. She had laughed, understanding that while she was pretty enough, it was not beauty that had attracted him to her. If he saw her now, he might not even recognize her. She had no illusions about her looks, she knew that she had already lost the bloom of her youth.

Jonathon Douglas was handsome, she supposed, with his dark eyes and regular features, but she was not interested in him in that way. That time was over for her, it had passed her by. But Jonathon might become a friend to her, might even be able to help her get news of her brother. If the ice was solid, she might walk to Wellesley Island so that she could talk with him again. He was a chaplain, so it would not be strange or unseemly for her to seek his counsel. She would have to extricate herself from the lies she'd told him, but he would understand the need to invent a husband and a protective father. She would tell him about Thomas MacGregor, who had been a proper schoolmaster, educated at St. Andrews in Scotland. She would tell him about her mother's family, the O'Neills, proud Donegal fishermen eight generations back, and about her twin brother Finn.

Even as she made the plans, she knew they were preposterous. She could not imagine hiking on the wind-scoured ice to the prison camp, making her way past all those poor men held under guard in the terrible cold. Reverend Douglas might misunderstand her intentions for coming. She ate another bit of the cornbread, packing away the rest in the tin. Then she went to her bed and retrieving the hawthorn box, carried it to the table, pulling the oil lamp close. She lifted one of the letters to her cheek. She didn't need to read it, she knew it by heart. After a moment she returned it to its rightful place. Then she opened the drawer in her table and pulled out a candle. It had been gnawed on the end by mice but would still serve its purpose.

On Christmas Eve in Kilcar, a candle was set in the window of every cottage to light the way for Joseph and the Virgin Mary. As soon as they had lit their own, Anya would insist that her mother hike with her and Finn along the lane to see the glowing windows and holly-festooned doors. Her mother in her periwinkle shawl, still young, laughing, singing carols with the twins in her clear sweet voice.

It startled her when such images appeared, vivid as if they'd happened that very day. She pushed the memory aside. Her mother, like Finn, had abandoned her, leaving her own daughter to make her way in the world without her. Anya set the candle in a jelly jar and placed it on the narrow sill. If her brother came in search of her that night, he would see the candle and know that she was waiting for him. Perhaps it would light his way home.

CHAPTER 8

City of Detroit

WHEN THE WHISTLE BLEW, Tom Kennedy checked his watch—the train from Buffalo was right on schedule. It had been almost two weeks since he'd last seen his brother. He was worried about Robbie, whose behavior had become increasingly erratic since the disaster in New York. He hoped that Rob had gotten the message that he was to meet him in Detroit, and that he was sober enough to catch the train. Tom would convince his brother to cross Lake Erie into Canada where they'd be less likely to be tracked. The uproar over the bombing plot had not died down. The Federals had made finding them their top priority.

Then Kennedy noticed the man he'd seen in a tavern just a few weeks earlier, Ben Young, advancing along the platform. Young looked focused, predatory, and he was accompanied by several men, their pistols drawn. They were detectives, Kennedy realized; his brother was stepping into a trap.

The locomotive screeched to a stop, emitting a cloud of steam, and his brother swung down the steps and onto the platform. Before Tom could call out, Robbie was surrounded by the detectives. There were too many of them, they were too well armed, and so Tom Kennedy ducked his head, stepping amidst a family gabbling in some foreign language, and made his way back into the station. From his position by the ticket counter, he saw his brother in handcuffs being led away. Robbie was now wrestling angrily with his captors, calling for help to the crowd around him, shouting that he was being kidnapped by Confederate spies. Tom followed at a distance, close enough to see his brother being pressed into a wagon with five guards. They would take no chances; this prisoner was worth his weight in gold.

Tom knew that when they searched Robbie, they would find a card identifying him as Thomas Cobb of Rock Island, Illinois. If they searched more thoroughly, they would find clues to his real identity sewn into the lining of his greatcoat, Confederate notes and maps of several cities in the North. The evidence would be enough to prove that they had captured Robert Kennedy, the most hated man in New York.

Tom Kennedy had met Ben Young at a roadhouse on the border near Niagara Falls, just before Christmas. There had been nothing remarkable about him. He sat down at the table next to Robbie and Tom, drinking in silence. After awhile Young introduced himself and got to talking about the war. He'd lost the hearing in one ear, that was all. Lucky, he said, with a bitter laugh. Didn't matter which side you were on, it felt like you were fighting just to stay alive. No cause was worth what he'd seen.

Then Robbie stood and swung at him, calling Young a bastard shite and Lincoln an ape, stumbling to the bar, challenging any man in the room to spit on the Union flag. Ben Young had watched for moment, then leaned toward Tom. "Your friend best shut up," he'd said in a low voice. "Spies everywhere." Then Young had departed. Tom had pulled his brother from the tavern and had forgotten all about the man.

Kennedy watched the agency wagon pull away, one of the remaining detectives shaking Young's hand in congratulations, clapping him on the back. In due time, he would kill Ben Young. It would be easy enough to find out his real name and where he lived, to dispatch him in his bed or outside some tavern. There was no particular rush. For now Tom Kennedy would be consumed by other business. He would follow Robbie to New York. He would study the prison layout, find out who took bribes. And Robbie would do his own part: he did not look like a hero, with his bandy legs and garrulous manner, but he had escaped Union prisons six times. He would do so again.

Then, together, they would sift through the clues about the fiasco in New York. Had their initial suspicion about the chemist been well founded or had a spy been planted in their group? This was more likely. They had been betrayed, that now seemed obvious, by one of their own.

CHAPTER 9

BY THE FIRST WEEK IN JANUARY, blizzards slammed the island, one after another, rolling downriver from Lake Ontario. The school had remained closed through Twelfth Night, and Anya was forced to accept the fact that she could not survive on her own. In such weather people froze to death overnight in their own cabins, even those who knew how harsh island winters could be. She found herself growing exhausted from the effort to stay warm, her muscles clenched against the cold. Her store of food was dwindling, and if she admitted the truth to herself, she was dangerously lonely.

So when Michael Burns appeared at her cabin with an invitation from his father, she didn't hesitate. His mother had fallen ill and needed help, and Anya could tutor Maddie, who missed her lessons. Michael waited astride his horse while Anya quickly collected her things. He hadn't realized that she lived out here alone. It was too isolated, there were too many rogues and roughnecks about. Then he watched her step onto the porch with nothing more than a half-filled satchel and clumsily board up the door. He should have helped her, he realized, but she obviously was used to doing for herself. He strapped her satchel to the pommel of his saddle, hauling her up behind himself. She sat stiffly, uncomfortable with their proximity, but when the horse took its first step she gripped him about his midsection to keep her balance, as if she were no more than a lass.

As they made their way up the path, Michael let the horse pick its way through the drifts. The sun had melted the crust but the warmth was deceptive. If the sky clouded over, it would fall below zero and the trail would turn to ice. He had brought his rifle in case a deer crossed their path, but he had seen no tracks along the way. Likely they would be browsing in the balsam forest further down the island. There wasn't time to check. As it was, it took most of an hour to make their way back to the farm in the deep snow, and they did not speak the whole journey.

The Burns farm was well-situated on a south-facing rise, protected on the western side by a thick stand of fir. As they approached the lane, the exhausted horse found new energy, and when they got to the yard, Maddie and Charlie burst out of the back door to greet them. A large shepherd mongrel barked importantly on the front porch.

"You took forever!" Maddie shouted. "We thought you'd never get here!"

Charlie laughed as Anya slid awkwardly to the ground, clapping his hands. Anya took her satchel from Michael and looked around. The farm was smaller than it looked from the road. A sagging ell connected the house to the barn, and snow drifted up to the eaves. A path was dug from the barn to the filthy paddock, where several cows huddled together for warmth. The old dog lumbered toward her, tail wagging.

"Laddie's just an old fool," Maddie said. "Don't mind him." She ruffled the dog's fur.

"Where is your father?"

"He's in the barn. Mama's having a rest." Then Maddie took Anya's satchel in a proprietary way. "Come in! Come see our room! Charlie's moving in with Michael."

Anya saw that it was a mistake to come. She had been so long on her own that she suddenly doubted her ability to endure their proximity, the dog, the brother and sister who greeted her so eagerly, Michael, who seemed uncomfortable with her presence. She thought of her cabin in the shadow of the pines, her precious collection of books, the pretty quilt on the bed. In her haste she had packed only a few things. At least she had her hawthorn box and her mother's shawl. Then she noticed

Maddie regarding her.

"It will be all right," Maddie said.

And so it was, in its way. The days were so filled with housekeeping that Anya hardly had time to dwell on her own situation. The chores seemed endless, but there was something comforting in the routine: Monday, laundry, Tuesday, baking, Wednesday, churning. Wood always to be chopped and stacked, water hauled, clothing mended. Cora made games out of the chores, singing Scottish ditties and teasing Maddie and Charlie.

"Everything takes twice as long, but I'd lose my mind if I didn't!" Cora said. "Angus and I are lucky to have our farm, I praise God for that, but…" She made a face, shoving her auburn curls from her forehead. "You know what I wish we had? A sailboat! I'd feel free as a bird in such a boat, as if I had wings!"

Anya smiled. Cora looked like Maddie just then, with her freckles and wiry frame. "My mother wanted to go out in the fishing boat with her da and her brothers, but women weren't allowed, they were supposed to bring bad luck."

"Is your mother still in Ireland?"

"No," said Anya. "She died before we left."

Cora nodded but didn't press her.

As the weeks passed by, Cora seemed to flag earlier in the day, retiring in the afternoon to her chilly bedroom, curtains drawn, door closed. At first Anya wondered if she were with child and having difficulty in that regard. The little cemetery in the glade held the stones of three wee ones. But if anything, Cora was losing weight, not gaining, and she wasn't making any preparations, sorting through infant clothes or setting up a cradle.

After supper, Anya and Maddie washed the dishes while Angus loaded the wood box for the night. Even with the stove stoked, the rest of the house remained cold, the west wind rattling the windows, unnerving the old dog. They remained in the kitchen, listening as Maddie translated passages in Latin from a battered volume she had brought from the school. Angus, who could not read or write, watched his daughter with mystification and pride. As a boy, he had worked in a manufactory in Glasgow before making the passage with Cora to America. Bright, his girl was. Learning Latin, like a laird's daughter. If they had stayed in Scotland she'd be stuck in a mill, never seeing the light of day except for an hour or two on Sundays.

Maddie focused intently on the lessons, impatient when she made mistakes, irritable with Charlie when he mimicked Anya's Irish accent or her own halting voice. Then her mother would laugh, pulling the boy close. "Maddie, don't scold, he thinks it's a game."

"He's five years old and still a baby. You are keeping him a baby!"

Although Anya said nothing, she had to agree. The boy was becoming unmanageable. Cora caught her expression and smoothed her son's hair.

"Next year he'll be off to school. For now, he's my laddie, my last one. When you have your own, you'll understand."

Charlie wriggled free from her. "Laddie's a dog!"

Angus spoke in a mild voice. "Charlie, you must be quiet so Maddie can study! Get the cat off the table."

But Charlie paid no mind, climbing onto the chair, kicking the rungs as he chanted the declensions.

Michael never joined them, yet his presence was so palpable he might have been pacing in the kitchen, not overhead in his room under the eaves. They listened as he moved back and forth, back and forth, first his step, then the crutches, in that small space. How trapped he must feel in his childhood room, Anya thought, looking at his old books and toys. She knew that his mother's concern would weary him most of all, because he could not offer what she needed most, the evidence that her son was sound, that the years of war had made no more difference than living away at school.

When Michael was out of the house, Cora spoke endlessly of him. "That boy was full of deviltry." She laughed. "Such a rascal! He broke his arm when he was nine, climbing a pine to catch a raven to tame. As soon as the arm was set, he climbed right back up again, wearing the splint. I thought his father would clobber him for sure."

Anya doubted that Angus had ever raised his hand to any of his children. He seemed almost perplexed by them, as if they weren't his, as if he wasn't quite sure how he had landed at this farm on Grindstone Island.

"Did Michael finally catch one?" It seemed like bad luck to her.

"He did. Its mother almost put Michael's eyes out. He named it 'Edgar' after a poet they read about in school." Cora snapped the linen she was folding, her voice suddenly sharp. "This war. That schoolmaster, the one who taught him the poem, he's dead. The Karlsons' beautiful son, dead. Nils was Michael's boyhood friend, he used to sit at our table." She reached to the topmost shelf and retrieved a tintype of Michael. She handed it to Anya. "I can hardly bear to look at it."

Anya took the likeness to the window where the light was better. In the tintype, Michael was little more than a lad, a farm boy, his mouth soft, his hair curling about his forehead. His eyes were bright, his expression filled with bravado, hope. She wouldn't have recognized him.

"Only seventeen when he enlisted. Came back from town strutting around the yard like a rooster. He was angry I wouldn't let him wear his uniform for his tintype like the other boys." Her voice rose. "He told his father before he signed on, and Angus didn't stop him, didn't tell me until it was too late. Next thing I knew he was fighting in Gettysburg. Can you imagine?" She paused. "I don't know if I can forgive Angus for that. He said that it was the right thing to do for the country. That he himself would go if he didn't have to keep up the farm." She pulled another piece of laundry from the basket. "Other farmers from Grindstone enlisted, and I believe Angus still worries that they think him a coward."

"I don't think you could have kept Michael from going." Anya twisted her mother's ring. "I couldn't keep Finn behind."

Cora looked at her then gently touched her hand. After a moment she continued. "When we came to this place, we had nothing, we knew nothing about farming, I was already with child. In all these hard years, Angus hasn't changed much. Even with all we've been through, our Michael off to war, the babies we lost, I can still see the lad in him." She stared at the likeness of her son. "But what happened to my boy?"

Her words frightened Anya. Would she recognize Finn when she saw him again? She felt a rush of anxiety, so strong she thought she'd lose her breath. She set the tintype back on the shelf. "I'll go now," she said hurriedly. "I'll see if…"

Anya pulled on an overcoat that hung by the door and stepped outside. She looked about the yard, almost blinded by the glint of sun on snow, then ducked into the barn. The place was cavernous, smelling of hay, warm with animal heat. At first she had trouble seeing in the shadowed light. Then she saw Michael, sitting on a barrel, methodically drilling holes in a wooden slab. When he looked up, she struggled to compose herself, wiping her eyes with her sleeve.

She cleared her throat. "I didn't know you were in here. I was looking for the children."

He noticed she was wearing his mother's overcoat. She was so thin, it hung about her frame like a cape. "They're off with their father delivering milk. Doesn't Mother need help?"

"She's resting." Anya saw that he was constructing a chair, twisting the ends of the chair-back into the holes. She remembered that Cora had asked for another one, now that Anya was living with them. To Michael, her presence must have simply meant more work. "I don't have any chores right now. I could help you with something."

"No need."

"I can help." Her voice was sharper than she'd intended. She started over again. "I know what it costs your father—all of you—to keep me."

He saw then that her eyes were wet with tears. "All right," he said.

"You can water the horses." He stood and grabbed his crutches, then led her to the stalls, where the horses stamped and snorted impatiently. "See that bucket? Fill it from the trough and set it inside."

"Go into the stall with the horses?"

"With the horses." He tried to make a joke. "Are you afraid of every four-legged creature that walks this earth?"

"There were no horses in Ireland," she said, her voice cold. "At least in our village. We ate them. The dogs as well." Then she stopped, ashamed. Her anger had come at him like a weapon.

Michael didn't say anything. He picked up an axe and went over to the trough. With one blow, he cracked the ice. Then he filled a bucket and handed it to Anya. "Come here," he said, opening the door.

After a moment, Anya approached him. He was murmuring to the horse, stroking its flank. "Horses don't like to be startled. Talk to her, touch her. Here. Don't be afraid." He awkwardly lifted Anya's hand, pressing it against Winnie's neck. Anya was so startled by his touch that she flinched, but when he removed his hand, she began to smooth the horse's thick winter coat, feeling it shudder under her palm.

Michael watched her, noticing how her dark hair fell down her back. He'd seen her wash it one time, drying it by the fire. Her cheeks were pale as milk. Then he saw how thin her wrists were, bird-like, skin stretched across the bones. On her right hand was a speckled burn that might have come from splashed lye or boiling water. A slash of a scar ran between thumb and index finger.

"It was the worst with the horses," he said quietly. "With the shelling and all. It wasn't right."

She did not look at him, but continued to stroke the horse, waiting for him to continue, but he moved away from her, setting the water bucket on the floor. The horse emptied the bucket in rapid gulps then Anya went to the trough to refill it for the next stall. Anya and Michael worked together in silence, and when they were done she set the bucket by the trough, wiping her hands on her apron.

"We didn't eat horses," she said finally. "Or dogs. In truth, our village was not as hard hit as most places." She paused. "And my grandfather was Scottish, he was the landlord. We didn't live with him but we never came close to starving. It was wicked of me to say so."

"Not so wicked."

"It was, because so many did."

Balancing on his crutch, Michael pitched some hay into the stall. "You said your husband was with the 94th. When did he join up?"

"Last spring."

Some good Irishmen in the regiment, better than what was said about them. He remembered them at night, after the fighting, sitting around the fire, playing cards, smoking and talking among themselves in Irish, their voices rising and falling like music. Joking after the worst of times.

"I haven't heard from him in a long time."

"Doesn't mean he's dead." Then he saw that Anya was taken aback by his brusqueness, and so he tried to keep the impatience from his voice. "It's hard to write letters."

"I understand that," she said. "I just – miss him."

Her sadness irritated him. She had no idea, none of them did, of what it was like. At first his father had tried to ask questions, but Michael finally explained that for him the war was over, he had already put it behind. His father had seemed relieved to let it go.

"Well, I'll go now to see about your mam," said Anya. "I can help you again tomorrow."

"Maddie will be back." He resumed his work, rubbing oil into the spindles of the chair back. Without looking at her, he said, "Thank you, Mrs. MacGregor."

"Michael, you must call me Anya. I'm younger than you. Even Charlie calls me that."

He looked up. "I'm not Charlie."

"I know that," she said, her voice mild. She turned and left the barn.

He listened as the door swung shut. He should have asked her about his mother. He knew that it had been hard for his mother to ask for help, that she hated relying on anyone else. Some days she seemed fine, and then she would seem to collapse before his eyes. It was likely some woman's problem, so he didn't want to question her, his own mother. He began to polish the chair with a rag; he would make it perfect for her, she rarely asked for anything.

When he'd first come home, she had made up her and his father's bed for him so he wouldn't have to climb the stairs. She pulled up a chair and sat by him all the while, even when he slept. Most of the time she didn't speak, just sat in silence letting him be. But on the third night, she finally brought it up. He saw the fear in her face.

"Are you in pain, Michael?"

"It's mostly healed up."

"Michael, they said that at Spotsylvania twelve thousand lads were lost, for the sake of a square mile of ground." Her hands shook as she had tried to smooth his coverlet. "That's the distance from here to the lane. How is that possible?" she whispered. "Is it true?"

He had closed his eyes, pretending to doze off, and finally she kissed him on the forehead and went downstairs.

A square mile, that was probably about right. At the Angle where he had fought, it was worse, the ranks lining up just yards apart on an acre or two of land. Going at it all day and long into the night in the rain, the whole damn war condensed in that small patch of mud. You couldn't move, couldn't get out of the way of the shelling, the rifle volleys. He remembered climbing onto a pile of bodies and hurling his bayonet like a spear into the mob, he could still feel the barrel in his hand. The Bloody Angle, they called it. He had seen the dead piled four layers deep in the muck and the mire, the wounded twitching and weeping beneath the corpses. But now, when he dreamed of it, he only saw that tree, that huge old oak, cut in half by the barrage of Minie balls.

CHAPTER 10

WINTER HAD SET IN with a ferocity that shook, then stunned him. After Toronto, Douglas had imagined himself prepared for a northern winter, but he had not expected a siege. It was the wind that most demoralized him, howling day and night, shifting the drifts around the hut. Some mornings he awoke to find his slit of a window totally obscured. In terms of camouflage, it perfectly suited his purpose. But by the end of January, he thought he would go mad.

So he hiked again across the ice to Grindstone. Finding game was harder than he'd expected; he'd had to settle for a couple of rabbits and an old turkey. And with the road heavily drifted with snow, he knew it unlikely that the school would be open. Still, he was disappointed to find it locked, the Irish woman's cabin boarded up. Where had she gone? Had she left the island altogether?

He pulled the board from the door and went inside. The placed was swept clean, cold as a tomb, but she obviously meant to return. Kindling lay ready in the hearth, and a summer cloak hung by the door. He decided to stay for awhile. There was no one about to see the smoke from the chimney, and he would be able to cook his game with efficiency and a measure of comfort.

From the outside her cabin was as rough as a hunter's lay-by, but she had added some feminine touches to soften the place, patchwork curtains, a faded rug, a jar of dried herbs on the table. Such details added pathos rather than comfort to the scene. The fireplace was so small as to be next to useless. A worthless muzzle-loader stood by the door. The cabin was almost as rude as the hovel where he himself would wait out the winter. Now that he knew how young she was, he wondered how she had survived the solitude for so long.

A few books had been stacked on the table next to a battered tin box. He had selected a volume of poems by an Irish writer he did not know, and lighting a candle, opened it and read the inscription.

1 March 1863
To Annie from Your Brother Finn

So the husband of whom she spoke was actually her brother. There was nothing in the cabin to suggest a husband. How much of what she had told him was actually true?

The poems were in Gaelic, translated into English. He skimmed the first lines.

I saw her once, one little while, and then no more:
'Twas Eden's light on Earth a while, and then no more.

He returned the volume to the shelf. The stack of newspapers looked worn; he hated to think about how many times she had read them. He looked at the dates—all were at least two months old, no information of any use to him. Then he opened the food box and found only a packet of tea. A summer skirt and a pair of trousers were carefully packed in lavender in the old trunk, along with a man's yellowed linen shirt. No pistol or ammunition, nothing under the mattress.

Annie MacGregor would be appalled to know that he had used her dish and cup, had spent several nights in her bed reading her few books and old newspapers. He had all but memorized the volume of poetry her brother had given her. Mangan was no Keats, half in love with easeful Death, but his words rang true:

Tell how this Nameless, condemn'd for years long
To herd with demons from hell beneath,
Saw things that made him, with groans and tears, long
For even death.

He himself had not come to that state, but he'd known men who had, indeed, longed for death, awakening in the delirium of pain, discovering that they'd lost a leg. How many limbs had he removed? Stacked like wood they would amount to a cord or more. He'd gotten good at it: he could get through a tibia in thirty seconds, a fibula in less, even by lamplight. He might have saved their lives, but the men never thanked him for it. They were so young that they saw no future for themselves as crippled men. He was more their enemy than the Federals who had turned their mortar on them.

As the west wind howled about the cabin, he read the girl's childhood journals, the ones that contained stories about her and her brother's adventures. He was oddly moved by her childish script.

Annie & Finn & the Power of Two

Annie & Finn went to the forest one morning & found a little red bird. "Tell us something magical," says Annie.

"I know where Aisling has gone. You must follow me." The red bird flew off. Annie was braver than Finn and so she made him come too.

The story went on for several pages, ending when they found Aisling safe in a fairies' bower. There were other stories, of the same sort, with Annie the hero, making her brother partake in some fantastic adventure. In one, she scolded Finn.

"You are only a clumsy giant with a magic salmon, but I am the QUEEN OF THE FAERIES! I have true magical powers and all of the faeries will do my bidding."

Annie had also been keeping a journal, with daily entries up until January 6th. It was little more than a collection of observations about the weather, the birds she'd seen, a few poor sketches. He flipped back to the 24th of December to see if she had made mention of him. There was a lengthy entry on Christmas Day, but it was written in Gaelic. He tried to remember what she looked like, sitting in front of the fire. It had been a month ago, and he had only an impression of a heart-shaped face, dark eyes and hair, her rich voice. A trace of her scent remained in her bed. She would be appalled that he knew her in that way.

He would allow himself to remain in her cabin for one more night. He had thought it would strengthen him to stay there, but it was having the opposite effect. He found the thought of returning to his camp unbearable. Worse, he was thinking about her, wondering where she was, how she was making her way. When he would see her again.

When the weather broke he would hike to Clayton and provision himself, purchase some newspapers. He'd been too long without news. Even though the war was all but lost, he had to know the particulars. He would have to find a way to send funds to his mother and sister; the merchant Brady might be bribed.

He knew that when the war ended, his fellow conspirators would come after him, but for now it was safe enough to remain in the islands.

He still had time to plan for the next step. Boston, perhaps, or Quebec, then on to Europe. He would write to his mother from there, try to explain his actions. His father would have understood his motives; he had never believed in slavery nor sanctioned the slaughter of civilians. He would not have forgiven, however, the betrayal of one's comrades.

CHAPTER 11

THE WEEKS PASSED SLOWLY, with a sameness that made Anya skittish. When the weather was bad, they were trapped inside, and Anya sorely missed the privacy of her cabin. She worried that if her brother returned, he would not be able to locate her; she wondered if Jonathon Douglas had stopped by the schoolhouse on one of his hunting forays. She would have liked to have talked with him again, but she had heard that the prison on Wellesley Island had closed. He might have been transferred to another one or perhaps he had returned to his home in Philadelphia. In any case, she would not see him again.

When the weather was grand, as it sometimes was, Anya and Maddie would strap on their snowshoes and hike across the lower pasture, following animal tracks "like the Mississaugus do," as Maddie said. Angus would harness Jack, the big draft horse, and pull them up the lane in the toboggan, setting them free at the top of the rise.

Anya hoped that Michael would come to accept her presence at the farm, and in his way, he did. He treated her as he did his family, with courtesy and distance. As the winter wore on, he became more reclusive, heading off after he completed his chores, returning after they'd gone to bed. Charlie's cot was moved to his parents' room, where they listened for Michael's return, listening as he made his way slowly up the stairs. His mother worried that he was drinking too much, off with rough companions. Through the floorboards, Cora's and Angus's voices rose up to the bedroom in the loft, Cora's so faint Anya and Maddie could barely hear it.

"You must speak to him, Angus," Cora said.

"The lads were his comrades in the 94th," Angus said. "It's better to be with his mates than pacing alone in his room."

"Papa's right about that," Maddie muttered, shifting under the covers. "It about drives me mad when he does that. Step-thump, step-thump."

"Maddie!" Anya pinched the girl's arm.

"I don't care," she whispered fiercely. "He's so different now. He's awful."

"We can't know what he's been through, Maddie. He needs more time."

"He's been back for five months! Why doesn't he try to use the leg that Papa got for him?"

Angus's voice continued to drift upstairs. "I think I'll take that pup I've been looking at. A hunting spaniel. Michael would love to train another dog. Laddie's too old to hunt."

"A puppy!" Maddie breathed. "Anya, I've seen it at the Robinsons! She's so pretty, with long legs and floppy ears and golden eyes. I'll call her Riley!"

Anya lay there in silence. A dog would not raise Michael's spirits! The damage was deeper than anyone could fix. When Michael was in the room, she could sense his anger smoldering beneath the surface. She understood something of what it cost to keep such anger under control.

Angus brought home the pup, but Michael showed no interest in it. One morning when Anya was in the barn collecting milk with Charlie, they found the dog whining miserably in a stall. Before she could stop him, Charlie let it out, and it ran to Anya, barking wildly, racing around her. The dog made for the bucket and began downing the milk in sloppy gulps.

"No!" she cried. "Stop!" She waved her arms ineffectually at the pup.

"No! Stop!" Charlie shouted excitedly, mirroring Anya's actions.

Michael's shout cut through the mayhem. They flinched at his voice, the dog cowering at Anya's feet. Michael looked at Anya with irritation and grabbed the trembling pup and returned her to the stall. Then he latched the door and turned to Anya. "Why did you let her out if you can't control her?"

Anya picked up the bucket. "Come along, Charlie. We'll give this to the piggies for a treat. I'll sing you a song, shall I?"

"Anya."

She turned to Michael in surprise. It was the first time he had said her given name.

"I'll take the milk. Might as well let the pup have it. Don't bother about it."

She set the bucket down. "Please yourself." She turned to go.

"Wait." He shoved his hair from his forehead. "I know it wasn't you who let it out of the pen." His voice was filled with resignation. "My father gave it to me as if I were as old as Charlie. I told him I didn't want another dog, but he thought he knew best."

"All right then," Anya said. "Come along, Charlie."

Michael watched as she left the barn holding his brother's hand. She bent down toward Charlie and in a moment they were singing, softly at first, then louder, some Irish ditty.

We had five million hogs and six million dogs
And seven million barrels of porter!
We had eight million bales of nanny goats' tails
In the hold of the IRISH ROVER!

Charlie swung his arms, shouting the last lines, all his misery forgotten.

Was she unaware of the effect she had on him? He watched her with Maddie and Charlie, shrieking as they flew down the hill on the toboggan, rolling over into a drift, laughing, her hair covered with snow. Nights were the worst, when he lay in the room next to hers in the loft.

Through the thin partition he could hear her and Maddie whispering together like sisters. When he came in late, he could hear her breathing as she slept, shifting under the bedclothes. Once he heard her weeping, softly, as if she would smother the sound. After two months under the same roof, he knew her.

One morning Angus asked Anya to travel with Michael to Clayton. They needed supplies, he said, and with the sledge runners repaired, they could make it across the channel in no time. Maddie and Charlie could use an outing, and Anya might enjoy an afternoon away from the island. Anya was as excited as the children: Brady might have news for her and she could leave word for Finn about where she was now living.

Before they departed, Cora gave Anya some banknotes folded into quarters. "Buy sweets for the children. And something for yourself, some ribbons for your pretty hair." Cora smiled fondly at her. "Red would go well with your dark hair."

"I'll get some for Maddie," Anya said.

"Maddie? You might as well drape them on the dog! You know she won't fuss with ribbons! No, they're meant for you." Cora paused. "And if you would stop at the chemist's, Anya. I wrote it down." She handed her a slip of paper. "Make sure Charlie doesn't lose his cap!"

Anya climbed onto the back of the sledge, settling between Charlie and Maddie under the heavy robe. Michael harnessed Jack, the big draft horse, and, placing his crutches on the seat, hauled himself aboard. Then they were off, up the lane and onto the island road. In February, the snow was well-packed by sledges, and they quickly made their way down to the river's edge. When Jack hit his stride, they flew along the ice, Charlie gripping Anya's arm, shouting with excitement. Anya was caught up in it all, laughing with Maddie as they hit a pressure ridge. Michael glanced back at her in surprise, then with a grin goaded Jack to greater speed.

How different the St. Lawrence looked in winter, a white expanse with as many sleds as there had been boats. As they approached Clayton, they could see a few children skating in the harbor below the quay, ice fishermen huddled next to their fire pots. Sleds and sleighs lined the shore, the horses tethered to pilings. Michael slowed Jack as they approached the landing and brought him to a halt.

"I'll head up to the granary," he said. "Meet back here. Don't be long, now. No dawdling."

"But that's why we came, we want to dawdle!" wailed Maddie. "We want to look in the shops!"

Michael smiled, catching Anya's eye. "All right, then, for a bit." He waited, securing the reins as the children followed Anya up the river bank to the village. He had thought he might enjoy accompanying them through the village, but when he'd seen the condition of the path, he knew he would have a hard go of it. He did not want Anya to watch him struggle with his crutches up the icy rise. It was time for the artificial leg, he realized. Lots of veterans used them now, getting around as readily as able men.

When Anya and the children reached the landing, she paused, pulling out her purse. "Maddie, your mother gave money for sweets. Do you know where to find a shop?"

Maddie snorted with impatience. "Corbin's store! You can see it from here –just past the sailmaker's loft!" She pointed to a large stone building that fronted the river.

"I'll meet you there in a quarter hour."

"Where are you going?"

"I have an errand for your mother. Just keep track of Charlie, and I'll be right back." She gave Maddie one of the notes. "Charlie, be a good boy, stay with your sister."

Maddie grabbed Charlie's hand and they were off. Anya watched them for a moment then hurried down the frozen path to Brady's Mercantile. She paused to read the casualty list tacked on the wall of the shop. The roll contained only two names, none from Grindstone. Then she flipped through the lists tacked behind it, dating back to November.

So many names, but not Finn's.

As she entered the store, she felt the warm blast from the stove. On such a cold morning, Anya was surprised to see that there was only one other customer standing at the counter. Even though he had his back to her, she saw at once that it was Jonathon Douglas. She felt her cheeks flush with pleasure.

"The book and music are a dollar. Hard to come by," Brady explained. "Got them from a gentleman's estate."

Douglas nodded.

Brady added up the figures while Douglas arranged the packages into a worn haversack. Then he pulled on a cap and slung the haversack over his shoulder. As he passed Anya, she looked up at him.

"Reverend Douglas!" she said shyly.

He smiled politely and left the store, the door bell jingling in his wake. Anya looked after him. It was Douglas, she had not been mistaken. Surely he had recognized her.

Brady watched the proceedings with interest. A story there—the lass looked vexed. He set aside his ledger. "Mrs. MacGregor! I've been waiting for you to appear in my store. It's been months!"

"You have a letter for me!"

"Aye. That I do." He pulled an envelope from the front of the box. "It looks like it's been to Galway and back."

"When did it arrive?"

"Just last week."

Last week! The envelope was unsealed and so grimy that it must have passed through fifty hands. But it was Finn's handwriting, clear as could be. Suddenly there was not enough air in the room to breathe.

"Here, lass," said Brady. "Come out back, where you can have some privacy." He'd already read the letter; a broken seal was as good as an invitation. He led the way to his kitchen, and swatting a cat from the table, pulled out a chair. "You just sit here, Missus. Take your time. Can you see all right? I'll put on the lamp."

"Yes, I'm fine." She wanted him to stop fussing, she wanted him to leave her alone. Anya fumbled with the envelope and removed the sheets of paper. Only two.

15 July 1864

Dearest Annie,

I have not received any more letters from you and so I worry about you. I am sure you have not forgotten me. I have not forgotten you.

I am writing this letter in Union Hospital in Washington. It is one of the better ones, although the surgeons and nurses are overwhelmed with our numbers. I will tell you now that compared to the others, my injuries are nothing, and that I will live to find you. Annie, I am no coward, and the first to stand by my mates, but if they try to send me back to the front, I tell you this: I will not go.

It was at Cold Harbor that I was cut down. In the afternoon it was, and I lay in the field for three days. I heard men die who could have been saved. No one came for us, Annie, Grant wouldn't call a truce, and finally it were my mates who pulled me out against orders, at risk of hanging.

Here I lie in a clean bed with white sheets, but I am still on the battlefield, listening to men dying of thirst in the June heat.

Finn

Anya read the letter three times, trying to find something of her brother's spirit that she could recognize. Even in the hardest of times Finn had not despaired that they would find a way to survive. But he had never before descended into hell. She felt as if she were suffocating. Her heart racing, she left the store by the back door, stepping into the cluttered yard, finding her way to the path to the wharves.

CHAPTER 12

ALTHOUGH IT WAS EARLY AFTERNOON, men and boys were wandering up and down the lanes. A group of laborers shouted to her as she passed by, and she pulled her cloak over her head, covering her hair. As she walked in the shadows, she saw some men in uniform or pieces thereof, trousers or a jacket carelessly buttoned or hanging open altogether. Some of the veterans talked quietly together before a bonfire. Some stood alone, watching the proceedings. A few seemed to be watching nothing at all. Where was her brother? He could be hanging about like one of these poor souls, lost and forlorn, in some village in Virginia. He might be anywhere. Perhaps he was already dead, and it was a letter from the grave.

"Lass? Are you hurt?"

She looked at the man who had stopped to help. She could see only that he was old and poor and smelled of gin. "Never mind," she said. "Thank you."

As she turned away, she was startled to see Jonathon Douglas standing in front of her.

"Mrs. MacGregor, please allow me to accompany you."

"He meant no harm," she said. "He was only being kind."

"I can see that. But you seem ill."

"I'm not."

"I apologize for my earlier rudeness," he said finally. "I was distracted. I did not realize it was you until I had left the store."

"It doesn't matter."

"Mrs. MacGregor, what has happened?"

When she spoke, her voice was shaky. "I got a letter from Finn. From hospital in Washington."

"Then you know he's safe."

"July he was there, *July*. He wrote that they would send him back to the fighting. Would they really do so?"

He took her arm. "Please, let's walk toward the village." They moved slowly together up the icy lane.

"I must go there myself, I must find him."

He stopped and turned her toward him. "Mrs. MacGregor, there would be no point. You would not find him."

She pulled away. "I would. I have funds, I could go there."

"You can't follow his regiment …it's not safe."

"I could be a nurse to the men. Women do that. I could work in hospital."

He was becoming impatient with her. "Mrs. MacGregor, the war is ending, the South cannot win. The soldiers will be coming north in waves, hundreds of thousands of men." He paused. "You must have faith that your husband will return."

"Faith. Yes. Well," she said. "Faith is your profession, Reverend Douglas." She turned to go.

"Annie."

She looked at him in surprise.

"Mrs. MacGregor, are you still living on the island?"

"You called me Annie. How do you know my name?"

He smiled. "You told me so, last Christmas Eve. Don't you remember?"

She looked at him uncertainly. Why would she have told him her childhood name? "Of course I'm still on the island. I live there with my family."

"Is the school still closed?"

"Until the big storms pass. The farmers say that when Lake Ontario freezes up the snow won't be as bad." She tried to smile. "Surely it must be frozen by now."

"I'm sorry for your bad news, Mrs. MacGregor. But you must assume your husband is sound, that you will see him again." He took her hand. "I'm certain that he will return to you."

She could see that he was trying to be kind. "Thank you. But I must be going now." She had forgotten all about the children. She withdrew her hand and hurried up the road to Water Street.

By the time Anya made it to the corner, Maddie was hugging herself with cold and Charlie was crying. "You took a long time," Maddie said.

"I'm sorry," Anya said. "Charlie, stop fussing. Don't be a baby." The medicine. She'd forgotten it. "Come along with me to the chemist. You'll warm up if we hurry."

"Who was that man you were talking to?"

"No one. A friend." She ducked into the shop. When she passed the note to the chemist, he looked at her briefly. "Laudanum. For pain?"

Anya looked quickly at Maddie, who was listening. "I don't know," Anya said. She paid the man then grabbed the children's hands and slid down the bank to the sledge.

Michael sat there watching them, stone-faced. "Why is Charlie upset?"

Anya didn't reply. She climbed aboard, settling between the children. Then Michael turned the sledge around and they were on their way back to Grindstone. The sky had clouded over, and the light had gone out of the day. Charlie wouldn't look at her, holding his arms tightly about himself.

"Charlie," she whispered. "Did Maddie buy you some candy?"

He nodded without looking up.

"What kind?"

He shrugged, his face averted, but pulled a packet from his pocket.

"Oh, these are grand. Lucky boyo."

"Boyo." He smiled.

Maddie was watching her closely. "Anya, who was that man you were talking to?" she whispered.

"No one," she said. "Don't make a fuss."

After a moment, "Why is Mama taking that pain medicine"

"I don't know."

Michael urged the horse onward. So Maddie had seen them as well, Anya and the stranger standing close together, talking intently. There was something between them, there was nothing casual about their conversation. He didn't like the man's looks, something off about him. His coat was filthy, ragged, but the boots were expensive. Even as the man spoke to her, he was looking around. Not restless, exactly. On guard. When the man realized that Michael was watching him, he slipped away, sinking into the shadows. He wasn't from the islands, Michael was certain of it. How did she know him? What was their relationship?

It didn't really matter. She would be gone as soon as the weather changed. His mother's illness was the real concern. She never made a fuss about pain, enduring a bad burn, a twisted ankle without so much as a shot of whisky. If she was taking laudanum, she was suffering more than he had realized.

When they got back to the farm, Anya sent the children into the house and waited in the barn as he pulled off Jack's harness and put the horse in the stall. He ignored her for as long as he could.

"Michael?" she said finally. "May I ask you something?"

He turned to her. Without speaking, she handed him an envelope. He looked at her, confused. Then he saw that her hands were shaking and that she was trying to compose herself. He opened the envelope and pulled out the letter.

"Do you know this place, Cold Harbor? Were you there?"

He scanned the pages, trying to read, but his own memories began crowding out the words. It had been such a quiet morning, a light rain falling softly as the men readied themselves, coming into position in the half-light before dawn. Many had pinned name tags to their uniforms,

78

knowing what was to come. When the heavy guns opened, the sound closed in on them, the whine and burst of the shells almost beyond bearing. As soon as the barrage ended they were supposed to go forward, crossing the open ground to storm the enemy trenches before the Rebels had time to recover. That was the theory, anyway. The men knew better, but there was nothing to be done about it.

And so it happened, just as they knew it would, the charge going forward, hitting a wall of flame as volley upon volley erupted along the length of the enemy lines. What followed were three days of suffering and regret, made worse by a folly of stubborn pride that defied all reckoning. Three days in which the weather cleared and the Virginia sun took up where the fighting had left off. What he remembered most from that time were the wounded men calling for help. And then the smell, a stench of death so powerful there was no getting used to it and no means of escape. On the third day Grant finally gave in, requesting a cease-fire to remove the dead and dying. By the time the litter bearers were finally allowed to go in, himself among them, they found only two men alive. The rest was digging, days and nights of digging in which the shovel became part of his hands, his only weapon against the overwhelming presence of death. By then they weren't burying men, just a putrid mass of decaying flesh. They did the best they could.

After a moment he tried once more, forcing himself to read the letter. He now understood that her husband had been there as well, one of the voices he had heard crying out in the night, forsaken by his own comrades. He carefully folded the letter, then put it back in its envelope, then returned it to her. She was looking at him, waiting for an answer.

"I was," he said.

After a moment she nodded and tucked the letter into her pocket. Saying nothing more, she touched his hand, then turned and left the barn.

When Douglas had left the store, the sun's glare had momentarily blinded him. He had ducked his head, hurrying past the women dawdling in front of the window display. When he was a block from the shop, he slowed his pace. He had purchased too much, spent too much money in one place. Merchants always remembered the customers who spend. The book and the music were mistakes. Too specific. Then Annie MacGregor had entered the store, mentioning him by name. Aliases created a trail; he had already used Douglas in Washington and New York. And it was obvious that the exchange had caught the storekeeper's attention. The Irishman was not as simple as he pretended to be.

It was down by the wharves that he had seen her again. She had been standing against a wall, staring at the ground as if she'd been struck. He realized even as he approached her that it was reckless to involve himself with her problems. There were many thousands of women like her, on both sides, who had lost loved ones. His own mother had lost a son.

Then he noticed the man with the crutches staring at him. He did not recognize the amputee, but it was clear that he'd caught the man's interest. It might have been only about Annie, but the reason didn't matter. The fact that he had been observed was dangerous in itself. He ducked into an alley then made his way downriver along the bank. The footing was awkward where the snow had drifted, but he would be less likely to be seen from the quay. From a distance he scanned the town pier, scrutinizing the tangle of sledges along the shore. Nothing unusual, as far as he could tell.

He made his crossing at Goose Bay, setting out onto the ice. The wind from the west had picked up and so he headed to Round Island, then Maple. He was not concerned about being followed; the tracks on the ice would have blown away as soon as he made them, but as he trudged to his cabin, he dragged a hemlock bough behind him, obliterating his footsteps in the deep snow.

The hut was dug into a bank in a dense stand of cedar, well camouflaged with pine boughs. The snow was now so deep that where it drifted it reached to the roofline, and he had to clear the small windows for visibility. This time of year, someone would have to be looking for it to find it. He pulled the branches from the door. Once inside, he bolted it shut then dragged the deer skins across the entry, for as soon as the sun set, the temperature would drop below zero. He lit the small stove, then the lamp, and opened his satchel. Removing the music and the books, he set them on the small box next to the deerskin-covered pallet. First the newspapers.

The war was all but over. The details were pitiful: Hood had lost Nashville to the Union army, and the casualties were terrible, the general resigning in humiliation. Now Sherman was turning his attention to the Carolinas, Uncle Billy, the northern papers called him, a name which belied his demonic nature.

"When I go through South Carolina," Sherman said, "it will be one of the most horrible things in this history of the world. The devil himself couldn't restrain my men in that state."

The Federals would soon be in Richmond. He hoped that his mother and sister had moved in with relatives. He read that the price of flour was now $450 dollars a barrel; they would be unable to survive on their own.

On the third page, he saw the notice:

City of New-York ~ Bombing Villain Robert C. Kennedy Condemned

The attempt to set fire to the city

of New York is one of the greatest atrocities of the age. There is nothing in the annals of barbarism which evinces greater vindictiveness. It was not a mere attempt to destroy the city, but to set fire to crowded hotels and places of public resort, in order to secure the greatest possible destruction of human life. He has not only been guilty of carrying on irregular warfare, in violation of the usages of civilized States in the conduct of war, but he has, by outraging every principle of humanity, incurred the highest penalty known to the law.

Robert C. Kennedy will be hanged by the neck until dead at Fort Lafayette, New York Harbor, on Saturday, the 25th day of March, just after the noon bell strikes.

He read the article a second time, then a third. Robbie Kennedy had been a fierce and loyal soldier for the Confederacy. Now he would give his life for that cause.

He himself would be safe until March 25th, for until then all of Tom Kennedy's efforts would be devoted to liberating his brother. Robbie would be under heavy guard; Fort Lafayette was considered as unassailable as the Bastille.

Robbie would be hanged, there was no doubt about it, and then Tom Kennedy would come after him.

Time and again he recalled the moment in Toronto when they had turned to him, awaiting his explanation. He had seen the shift in their expressions as he clumsily defended himself, he who had always been so facile with words. And now Kennedy and the rest would put it together that it had been he who had betrayed them. Kennedy would hold him accountable for his brother's execution. And Kennedy would be right. He had betrayed them, not once but twice. All they lacked was the proof, and they would proceed without it. Tom would have no trouble getting the funds to buy information, enlisting loyal cutthroats to support him.

He set down the newspaper and fed more logs into the stove. The room was smoky, and so he tacked open the window flaps. What kind of a trail had he left behind? They'd last seen him in Toronto. Thompson would assume that as a good son, he would have made his way back to Richmond to care for his mother. They might assume that because he had family connections in Baltimore and New Orleans, he would move on to another city.

Even if they pursued his trail along the St. Lawrence, they would lose him in the islands. The area was filled with transients crossing the borders of both countries, and he had done little to attract attention to himself. His comrades would question the shopkeepers, of course. Brady would play his cards close to his chest, but even if money changed hands, Brady would have little enough to tell, only that someone who looked like him had been in the area. They would certainly not connect him to an Irish girl who lived on Grindstone. He would leave the islands as soon as the river broke up, heading to Nova Scotia, and then to France.

CHAPTER 13

BY MARCH, THE STORMS that rolled down from Lake Ontario began to abate. Although the fields would be snow-covered for another month, Angus was already planning his spring crops. With the longer days, Anya had re-opened the school, but she continued to board at the Burns's farm. Cora's health had worsened, and Anya knew that her help was needed more than ever. Cora moved carefully now, her face set, guarding against pain. A few times she lashed out at Angus for some small matter, and the children began to watch her closely. Michael made more frequent trips to Clayton, and when he returned he would enter his mother's bedroom, closing the door after himself. After awhile he would head out to the barn. His mother slept more soundly, then, and Anya knew she was using more laudanum. When she was cleaning, she'd found a number of bottles in the top dresser drawer. She opened one, sniffing the contents, and felt her throat begin to close. Her mother had smelled like that, toward the end.

Only once did Cora speak of the matter. The children were in the barn with their father, and they were alone in the kitchen, Cora wrapped in a blanket by the stove, Anya scrubbing carrots for supper.

"You're a good girl, Anya."

Anya looked at her, surprised.

"Come sit with me for a moment."

Anya set the cutting board on the table and slid onto the chair. She was frightened of what Cora would say.

"You know, when you came to the island, I worried about you. No kin, your husband gone off to the war. All alone in that cabin! ".

"You needn't have worried, Mrs. Burns."

"I can see that. You're making your own way in this world. But I'm grateful you came to stay with us, Anya. It means a lot, especially to Maddie. You've been a big help to us all." She watched Anya chop the vegetables. "Use the other knife, dear. It's sharper." She slowly stood and retrieved it from the drawer. "Maddie always wanted a sister, and she was crushed when Charlie was born. When Michael left for the war... well, she missed him terribly."

"Maddie is very bright," said Anya. "I am only one step ahead of her, you know. I wish she could attend a proper school."

Cora pulled the quilt around herself. The stove was fully stoked, but she couldn't seem to get warm. She was so quiet that Anya thought she had fallen asleep in the chair. Moving to the pump, Anya filled the pot with water and vegetables and set it on the stove.

Then Cora spoke again, her voice low. "When I left Scotland, I knew I would never see my mother again. I was sad to leave, of course, but I had Angus and thought I was on a great adventure. I didn't know then what 'never' would feel like. I missed her so, especially when I had my babies. I miss her even now." She paused. "And now I think about what my own mother must have felt saying goodbye to her children. It's time I tell my own and it's hard to find the words. They're so young."

Anya looked at Cora. The woman had aged so much it was hard to imagine that she had born a child just five years earlier. Anya felt a weight on her heart, and it took all of her steeliness to return to the table. She wanted to fly out the door and run all the way to her cabin. Instead she sat down and clasped her hands together.

"Anya, you told me your mother passed before you left Ireland but you never said how she died."

"She was ill." Anya cleared her throat. "A few years after our little sister died, our mam became ill and... she drowned." She twisted her ring.

Cora was silent for awhile. "I see," she said finally.

"I used to think it was only that she didn't want to leave Ireland, that our mam loved home more than she loved us." Anya paused. "A sailor told me that a body could die of homesickness, some even jumped overboard before they got to shore. He said he'd seen it happen on every crossing. So I thought that was why she left us. But now I believe it was because of her illness, she was worse off than we thought."

"A mother does not want to worry her children."

Then the words came in a rush. "I was a grown girl, and my mother didn't tell me. She must have thought me weak. Or selfish." Tears filled Anya's eyes. "But I could have helped."

Cora touched her hand. "No, dear, you couldn't. It's a private matter, this business." After a moment, "You mustn't blame your mother, Anya. Or yourself."

"Does Angus know?"

"Oh, Angus." Cora smiled. "Surely he knows, but we don't speak of it. He'd mourn for me before I was even gone, while I was standing right next to him washing up his dishes! I couldn't bear it, seeing his long face. He'd be a nuisance and I'd say something sharp and hurt his feelings."

"Michael knows."

"Aye, of course he does. And I will tell the children in my own way." Tears filled her eyes. "They are just too young to lose their mother, Anya. That's what I feel so terrible about."

Anya took Cora's hands in her own. "They will get through it, Cora. Don't worry. They have one another."

"They have you as well, Anya. And you them."

Anya nodded. They sat for awhile and when Cora fell asleep, Anya gently extricated her hands and covered her friend with the quilt. She went to the cook stove and put some kindling into the firebox and finished making supper.

The day Cora died, the world turned to ice, a late March rain freezing as it fell. The trees groaned and strained under the load, and the night was filled with cracking, like pistol shots, as one after another the great boughs broke under the strain. Angus left his wife's bedside to herd the cows into to the barn where they crowded together with the horses. Michael was away.

"Off to see his boon companions," Maddie said bitterly. The girl watched for him from the kitchen window, furious. "He worried Mama so and now she's dead."

Maddie looked a lot like Michael, Anya thought, eyes narrowed, mouth compressed. "It's not his fault, Maddie. Your da said that Michael was with your mother before he left this morning."

"My da? It sounds like baby talk. Is that what you called your father?" She pulled away.

Charlie stared at his sister, wide-eyed, silent. Anya let her be. She loaded the stove, then poured warm water into the basin. "You stay here with Maddie, Charlie. I'll call you when it's time."

It was left to Anya to prepare Cora for her final rest. Angus put it to her awkwardly, for it seemed a lot to ask, but in the storm there were no other women about, no other family. Anya didn't mind. She was glad to help Cora Burns on her journey, as she had not been able to help her own mother. Cora's final weeks had been brutal, frightening. She had begun to pluck at her bedclothes, groaning in pain, speaking to people in the shadows of the room. The night before she died, Michael must have increased her dose of laudanum for Cora finally fell into a heavy sleep. If that had helped her on her way, Anya was grateful.

As Anya collected the soap and linens for the ritual, she understood what happened to her mother, as if she'd been there to witness it herself:

One winter morning a few weeks before their departure for America,
Katherine O'Neill MacGregor left her wedding ring and a note on the table
by the window, then climbed down onto the rocks below the seawall. She
chose a place where the currents would carry her well away from the village,
for she knew what a body looks like just a few hours in the water. She knew,
as well, that as a suicide, she would not be allowed burial in the cemetery,
and while she did not mind for herself, she minded for her family. Steeling
herself against the cold, she waded into the dark waves, her skirts tugging
against her legs. She closed her eyes and leaned into her fate, and as she sank
her gown floated about her and she was lifted up by the merrows, the sea
women, and bourn out to sea.

Anya wept as she washed Cora's body, then wrapped her in her
dowry sheet, the one with the thistle embroidery she had brought from
Scotland in her dowry trunk. Anya brushed Cora's springy auburn hair,
which even now had only a few strands of grey. "*Go mbeannaí Dia duit.*
Codladh sámh," she said, then in English, so Cora would understand.
"May God bless you, Cora. Sleep well."

Charlie knocked again then opened the door. "I want to come in,"
he whispered.

"Aye, Charlie." Anya opened a quilt and pulling it over herself,
moved to the rocking chair. Charlie would not approach his mother's
bed, but instead climbed onto Anya's lap as if he were a baby. She let
him be. It was very cold in the room, so she pulled the quilt about
him. She was glad that Cora looked peaceful, her pain departed. Charlie
would not be frightened by the sight of her.

Had her spirit managed to escape? When Cora died, Angus had
covered the mirror, but it took him several minutes to open the window,
frozen in the storm. He pounded at the frame, so desperate that her soul
be set free that Anya thought he would break the glass. She was startled
by the scratching at the door but realized that it was only Laddie anxious
to be with his mistress. She gently set Charlie aside and opened it. The

old dog shoved his way into the room and slumped on the floor in his usual spot. Maddie was standing by the stove, poking at the fire.

"Your mam's ready," Anya said.

After a moment, Maddie went past her into the bedroom. Anya removed the basin and linen and returned to the kitchen, then scooped some warm water from the kettle and washed her arms and hands. She glanced at the clock, but it had been stopped when Cora died, as was the custom, so her spirit would not be distracted from its journey.

Then she heard the sound of hooves. From the kitchen window, she saw Angus standing by the barn door, holding the lantern to light Michael's way. She went upstairs so that he would not have to face her when he entered the kitchen.

By the next morning, the storm had passed, and the landscape glittered in the bright March sun. The snow was crusted with ice, and they could not walk about without slipping. Charlie sat with his mother's body while Anya and Maddie helped Angus lead the cattle outside, their breath filling the brittle air with clouds of vapour. They could hear from the rise the crack of the axe hitting frozen ground as Michael prepared his mother's grave. He'd been at it for hours.

"I told him we could wait for a thaw and a proper burial," said Angus, "when the people from church could say farewell. But he'll have none of it. He thinks it indecent to have her above ground."

Even with the storm, word somehow traveled about the island, and before dusk a small group gathered to pay their respects to Cora Burns in the little cemetery above the house. When spring came, the glade would be filled with wildflowers, but on this wintry afternoon the place offered small comfort to the bereaved. Maddie stood next to her father, shoulders stiff, cradling a bunch of evergreen boughs in her arms. She wore her mother's coat, which dragged on the ground in a way that twisted Anya's heart. Then Angus and some neighbors appeared, bearing Cora's coffin. Michael followed behind, his face haggard with grief, dressed in his Federal uniform. It startled Anya to see him so transformed, making real the cause of his injury. They set the coffin on the ground then lowered it into the grave. The assembly began to sing, in voices halting and ragged.

Nearer, my God, to Thee
Even though it be a cross that raiseth me,
Still all my song shall be nearer, my God, to Thee.

Though like the wanderer, the sun gone down,
Darkness be over me, my rest a stone.
Yet in my dreams I'd be nearer, my God, to Thee.
Nearer, my God, to Thee.

Then Maddie began to place her evergreens on the coffin lid, arranging them carefully, layering the top with balsam and winterberry.

"Not now, dear," said Mrs. Robinson, not unkindly, touching her on the shoulder. "Wait until after the minister sprinkles the dirt. The dust-to-dust part."

Maddie jerked away. "I don't want dirt touching my mother." She continued with her task.

After the burial was completed, the islanders proceeded to the farmhouse to show their respects. A fire had been laid in the parlor, and the crowded room finally grew warm, fogging the windows. The table was laden with food brought by the neighbors, and Maddie assumed the role of mistress of the house, awkwardly offering a platter to the guests. Anya saw her stiffen when someone tried to comfort her. "A blessing it is that the Lord took her, Maddie. God is merciful."

"Merciful?" Maddie's voice was high.

Anya pulled her into the kitchen. "You don't have to stay and listen to that."

Maddie ducked her head and bolted out the door, heading to the barn. Likely Michael was there as well, finishing some project, chopping wood, swinging the axe over and over so that the dull thud would become the rhythm of the night.

Angus was sitting in a chair by the fire, Laddie at his feet. "He keeps looking around for Cora," he said. "He'll wear himself out." Instinctively Anya reached over and patted the old dog, who peered up at her, then looked away. After a few moments, Angus spoke. "Cora was grateful for what you have given to Maddie. Cora wanted so much for our girl to read and write. I thank you as well."

Gazing at the flames, she wondered if Cora's spirit was with them now, sharing in the proceedings. The day Anya's mother died, her spirit returned to their cottage before she began her journey to the other side. They knew she was with them, although they did not see her shadow. They sensed her sitting with them in her rocking chair by the hearth. Katherine's spirit lingered for three days, and then her essence left, leaving them behind to struggle with their grief and confusion.

When her father died, where had his spirit gone? Had he wandered about the strange and filthy streets of Kingston or had he returned to their empty cottage by the sea? Anya worried that her father's face would soon fade from memory. Even now it was coming back only in bits, his eyes, his brow, but not in its entirety. And Finn's was disappearing as well. She didn't even have a soldier's tintype; they'd had neither money nor time for such a thing when he left for the war.

Chilled, Anya moved closer to the fire. Padraig O'Malley's tales were filled with death and the afterlife, about the faeries and wee ones who inhabited the forest. When she was a child, it was the banshees who had frightened her most, especially the one who appeared in a shroud, with the still-growing hair of the dead. If Finn were dead, would his spirit come to her in this forsaken place or would it look for her in their cottage in Kilcar?

She went into the parlor and began to collect the platters of food. Her brother was not dead, it was a betrayal to think so. It was just that her world had grown that much smaller with Cora's death, a light extinguished. She had not expected it to strike her so hard.

CHAPTER 14

THE PRISON CELL was heavily guarded, Kennedy under constant watch. He had already tried to escape, stabbing a man in the neck with a piece of his tin plate. It would not be long now. Robbie had been condemned as a monster, and in just a few hours, at the age of thirty, he would be hanged.

Tom had bribed his way into the crowded prison yard. He would not be recognized; he and Robbie looked nothing alike, himself a full six inches taller than his brother. He hoped that Robbie knew that he was there, that he would not let his brother die alone, among these despised people.

Then the door opened and a small group of officials processed into the yard. There was Robbie, his brother, Robert Cobb Kennedy, hardly diminished in the grey prison uniform, carrying himself with the bearing of a soldier of the Confederate States of America. The guards marched closely beside him as he mounted the scaffolding. Robbie bowed his head briefly in prayer as the priest gave his final blessing. Then Robbie lifted his head and shouted in a clear voice,

Trust to luck, trust to luck,
Stare Fate in the face
For your heart will be easy
If it's in the right place.

The startled guard pulled the hood over Kennedy's head, and when the signal was given, the trap door fell away, and Robert Cobb Kennedy dropped into the void. Seconds later it was over.

Tom Kennedy made his way back to the Five Points. In his greatcoat pocket were the packets that he would send to their family in Louisiana. They contained Robbie's likeness, taken two days earlier, and some locks of his hair. In the tintypes, two days before his execution, Robbie looked composed, clear of purpose.

He passed a newsstand and picked up one of the papers. There, on the front page was an illustration from *Harper's Weekly* that had been reprinted countless times since his brother's arrest.

"These Yankees will learn what it is to incur the Enmity of a proud and chivalric People."

Through all of the torturous questioning he had endured, Rob Kennedy had never given up a name. He was the very model of bravery, of pride and chivalry, the values the northerners derided. A loathsome people, they knew nothing of honor.

Nor did the man who had betrayed them. While waiting for his brother's execution, Kennedy had lain awake at night pondering the matter. He had questioned all of the shopkeepers and hotel clerks they'd dealt with. He had returned to the chemist and held a knife to the man's throat. Kennedy was now certain that it was the doctor, the man who called himself Jonathon Douglas, who was responsible for their betrayal. Not once, but twice, Kennedy was now certain, first with the election, then later, with the Greek fire.

And so he himself would track Douglas down and kill him, without dignity or ceremony. It would be an act without mercy, for his brother had not been allowed the same.

Kennedy would never rid himself of the image of his brother's last moment. He would never allow himself to forget.

He walked the streets, unaware of the cold. Where would Douglas be hiding? If he read the newspapers, he would know that Robbie had been executed. He would know that his own life was now worth nothing. They had allowed him to slip away in Toronto, in deference to Thompson, but it had been a mistake. He now had a four month advantage. He might have gone to Detroit, but that seemed unlikely, too many spies. He would be safer in Canada, passing himself as a Yankee. Maybe Douglas intended to wait there until the end of the war, then go to his mother and sister in Richmond. Kennedy had already posted spies in Virginia; they would know if his family was preparing to make a move.

Kennedy would gather some loyal men then begin the search in Toronto. If they found no information of worth in that city, they would head to Ottawa, then down the canal to Lake Ontario. Kingston was a possibility; he might have found work in the hospital there. Just below Ontario was the long stretch of islands where a man might believe he could hide forever. But Douglas would be deceiving himself. Kennedy would find him even if it meant combing the thousands of islands one by one.

CHAPTER 15

A FEW WEEKS after Cora was buried, Anya moved back to her cabin. Truth be told, Anya could not bear the sadness of the household. It filled her with guilt to leave the children, but she felt so weighed down that she seemed unable to lift her own spirits, let alone theirs. And something had shifted in Michael, something dark had descended upon him, and at night she heard him crying out in his sleep, his voice so filled with horror that she lay awake with a pounding heart.

During the day he seemed more intent on avoiding her, and she thought he might do better if the family sorted things out on their own as they adjusted to Cora's death. So Angus filled a sack with food and reluctantly drove her back in the sledge.

The day was warm, the sky deep blue, and melting snow was falling in clumps from the pine trees. Charlie and Maddie climbed out of the wagon and stamped a trail to the porch in their snowshoes, then another down to the shore. With the axe, Anya pried the board from the door and swung it open. Snow had sifted onto the floor through the chimney but otherwise, all was as she had left it. She lit the kindling, and soon the fire began to snap.

Maddie helped her father carry the sacks of food into the cabin, then they brushed the snow off the woodpile and Angus split a stack of logs with the axe he'd brought with him. As Anya tied back the curtains, Maddie looked about in dismay. It was only one room! Why would Anya want to live in such a lonely place when she could live with them in a real house? With their mother gone, they needed her more than ever.

It must have been something Michael had said. Her brother watched Anya when he thought no one was looking. Then when Anya looked up, his expression would become hard. It angered Maddie that he had somehow driven Anya away. When she thought about it, she knew she would rather have Anya as a sister than Michael as a brother. But the choice wasn't hers, she had no say about anything.

"It's freezing in here, it's horrible," she said. "Come back with us, Anya. Don't stay here. You'll be cold and lonely. And there are probably mice." She couldn't bring herself to say how much she would miss her friend, how sad the farm would seem without her.

Anya smiled. "There are lots of mice in the farmhouse, even with the cats!" She smoothed the girl's hair. "You were kind to share your room with me all this time."

"Better than sharing with Charlie!"

"I left you my lavender water. And we'll see each other at school almost every day, you know that. We can have our dinners together."

Maddie shrugged. "I could bring biscuits. You can't bake anything here."

Then Angus was at the door. "Sister, time to go home. Charlie." He was carrying another load of wood. "Mrs. MacGregor, are you sure you want to stay here? It's the end of the earth! You don't even have a dog to keep you company."

"Mr. Burns, you've given me too much! I've more than enough. And I will be busy with school."

His face was filled with concern. "It doesn't sit well, missy. You should live with us, you are kin to us now."

Maddie and Charlie began to clap their hands. "You'd be my sister," Maddie said.

Anya felt herself wavering. "Thank you, Mr. Burns, but I must stay here. It's the life I made for myself…" She stopped, not knowing quite what she meant to say.

"All right, then," he said briskly. He turned and hiked out to the sledge, and returned with a shotgun. "This was Michael's as a lad. You should have it. And you can always change your mind."

Anya stood on the porch, waving as the sledge made its way up the path. When she heard Jack's hooves on the bridge, she felt a flash of panic. She had made a terrible mistake. How would she live alone again in this wild place? The night stretched ahead, cold and empty. She stepped inside and closed the door. She added more logs to the fire, then paced about, willing the room to warm. Unpacking her satchel, she set the letter box under her mattress then lined up the jars of preserved vegetables on the shelf. How strange—Cora had prepared them the previous summer, before Anya had come to Grindstone. And now, just nine months later, Anya was mourning Cora's death. She saw her friend standing by the kettle in the summer kitchen, wiping her hands on her apron, shoving her curls from her forehead. Slowly turning to smile at her.

"Cora? Are you here?" Tears filled Anya's eyes. How she wished they'd had more time.

As the cabin grew warm, Anya remembered that she would need water before morning. She strapped on her snowshoes, making her way down the path already set by the children. The snow was very deep, waist-high, camouflaging familiar features in the landscape. Ravens called from the pines, giving notice of her presence. Perhaps the little cat had survived and would return now that Anya had come back. The bright sun belied the chill in the air; although the farmers were already getting their seeds in order, spring seemed far away.

When Anya reached the river, she slid down the bank and made her way to the shore. Ice slabs had piled on top of one another, shoving boulders aside, transforming the shoreline. The river stretched before her, a highway of ice, windswept, deceptive; she knew that despite the cold, springs bubbled up here and there, keeping the ice spongy. She set down her buckets and began to chop a hole for water. She might drop a fishing line, if she could summon the patience to wait for a strike. Then she saw someone in the distance making his way toward her across the ice. The man moved quickly, his loping stride somehow familiar, and for a moment Anya thought he must be her brother. God had finally answered her long-ago prayers. Then, as if noticing her, the traveler stopped. After a moment, he turned away, quickly heading south, toward the Clayton mainland. Soon he was out of sight.

Anya angrily swung the axe, chopping at the hole in the ice. Wait for him, they said, all of them. Be patient. What sort of a philosophy was that? She swung again. The war was not over, it ran on and on, and lads were still killing one another. She shouted a curse as the axe slipped in her grip, slamming into the ice near her foot. She set the axe down, catching her breath. If she made another mistake like that, she might die right here on the ice. Who would help her, she thought bitterly, the mystery man who had turned away at the very sight of her?

Anya made her way back to the cabin, spurred on by her anger, and set the buckets by the door. The shadows had turned to darkness, and Anya lit the oil lamps, noting that they, like the woodpile, seemed more depleted than she had left them. In her absence had someone been using her cabin? As Anya felt fear seeping through her, she scolded herself. The place was just as she had left it, the kindling set, the floor swept, the corners sprinkled with mint to foil the mice. She would not allow her imagination to run unchecked. She had learned to be alone and she would do so again. She bolted the door and drew the curtains, setting the shotgun by the bed. It was small, a lad's gun, but better than the rusted one she hadn't even bothered to hide.

Anya folded back the quilt so the bedding would warm, and it was then that she found the book, a small volume caught beneath the bedclothes. She did not recognize it as her own and, heart pounding, she carried it over to the lamp. It was a book of poems by John Keats. It was not hers, of that she was certain. Feeling sick, she realized that someone had been in her cabin, had slept in her bed. Panicking, she looked about the room but saw nothing out of place. She sat at her table and opened the cover. There was an inscription.

29 September 1862
from Jakob

No tramp or trapper had visited her cabin. Whoever it was had left something precious behind. Anya blew out the lamp and closed her eyes, willing herself to sleep.

He made his way onto the ice, testing it with a long pole he had stashed in the woods. He would no longer risk a trip after dark. A few nights earlier he had been hiking back with supplies from Gananoque and, lost in thought, had come upon a patch of open water. A few more steps and he would have drowned.

The supplies would keep him for another few weeks, and then he would have to secure a better boat. He had already salvaged an old sailing dinghy. He had spotted it when he'd first arrived, the boat overturned, shoved against a bank on Picton Island. He had dragged it across the ice and hidden it under pine boughs. Although it was sound enough for the islands, the boat would be slow. When the ice broke, he would order one of the fast new skiffs now being built in Clayton.

He knew by the daily trail of smoke above the schoolhouse that school had been back in session, but he had not wanted to encounter Annie again. He knew too much about her and thought of her too often. When he saw her by the shore, he recognized her at once, even from a distance, and he had resisted the urge to go to her, to watch her eyes widening in recognition. He had turned away from her, heading downriver along the ice.

He made his way along the main channel before cutting back to Maple. The sun was higher in the sky, winter was turning to spring.

How long would he be safe in these islands? The appointed day for Kennedy's execution had passed. Tom Kennedy would certainly have been there, somehow he would have breached the prison walls. If he could not help Rob escape, if he himself was not caught in the attempt, he would have witnessed his brother's execution by hanging.

He assumed they would then begin their search in Toronto, scouring conversations from months earlier, questioning servants, hostlers, innkeepers. They would carry a likeness of some sort, sketched by some itinerant artist on the basis of Kennedy's excellent memory for details. They would show the portrait in the pubs and by the docks, using a story that would evoke sympathy: a missing brother, a comrade who'd lost his wits in the war. Eventually someone would recognize him.

He would not allow himself to be trapped in his lair like an animal. Although he was well-armed, it was absurd to think he could take on the lot of them. Better to plant a false trail, directing them south. The storekeeper, Brady, would be useful in that regard, he would go there again and leave a forwarding address in Philadelphia. Then he would stop in some of the other Clayton establishments, scattering details; he would register for a night in one of the hotels under the name he'd used in New York, Jonathon Douglas.

And there was Annie MacGregor. If they found their way to Grindstone, they might question her—the local schoolmistress might well have seen him. And if they questioned her, she would recall that he had spoken of Philadelphia, it might throw them off, at least for awhile. They would not harm her, for it would be obvious that she had no relationship with him. He did not worry about his mother's and sister's safety: Thompson would not doubt his family's loyalty to the Confederacy and would not countenance that sort of retribution. Tom Kennedy had honor, in that respect. He would not harm someone loyal to the Southern cause.

CHAPTER 16

SPRING HAD COME to northern New York and the world was green again, at least around the edges. The ice had broken up and the river was on the move. Great flocks of geese filled the marshes, and barges bound for Kingston and Toronto passed through the islands, loaded down to their decks with goods from abroad.

The war was over.

The day of the surrender, the church bells in Clayton rang so loudly that they could be heard on the island. Anya closed the school and joined the jubilant crowd that packed onto the ferries headed to the mainland. The river was filled with boats of every kind, horns and whistles blowing, and the village of Clayton was lively with bonfires, fiddlers, pipes and drums on every corner. Bunting was draped on the rafters and porch rails. Children raced about the streets, gathering in knots then breaking away in all directions. The mayor of Clayton made speeches and some of the older veterans gathered in impromptu parades. The townspeople were proud that their own 94th was at Appomattox that very day to witness Lee's surrender. Their sons and husbands had fought in some of the most brutal battles of the war, and now they would see history being made. And then they would come home. A few months more, Anya was told, but not to worry, her husband would no longer be sent into battle.

Anya had come to town with Angus and the children; Michael had gone earlier with his mates. As they made their way along John Street to the village square, Charlie raced about like a wild animal, but Maddie walked quietly by Anya's side, watching the proceedings as if from a great distance.

The girl had shadows under her eyes, and her mouth was tight; her hair was matted and her clothes smelled sour. When Angus stepped into the feed store, Anya asked the girl how things were going, and Maddie just shrugged and said they were getting by. Michael was likely to move to Clayton for paid work so that he could help with the expenses. A foolish idea, Maddie said, for her father needed Michael's help to make the farm go. She would have to take on his chores, it wasn't fair. Worse, she would have to bring Charlie to school with her, for with Angus trying to keep up with all the work, there was no one to mind him at home.

But the war was over. It had gone on for so long that Anya had begun to believe there would be no end to it, that she would spend her whole life waiting for news of her twin. She hugged herself, looking about the crowded square. She imagined him making his way to her, pushing through the crowd, shoving his hair from his forehead. Grinning, laughing with disbelief when he saw her. Annie MacGregor, he'd shout. You look terrible! What have you been doing all this time? He'd swing her in his arms and the terrible year would fade away almost as if it had never happened.

Three days later, the weather was unusually fine and her pupils restless, so Anya let them play outside while she sat on the schoolhouse steps. Closing her eyes, she could smell the coming of spring in the newly muddied earth. The snow had receded from the yard, although there were still deep drifts in the woods where the children could find snow to pack for weapons. The snowball fight was gaining too much energy, and in a moment she would stop the battle before someone got hurt.

Then they heard a cannon detonate from the mainland. Over and over it boomed, until Anya felt the percussion reverberate in her chest. A few of the younger children scurried to her and clung to her skirts.

"Are the Rebels here?" one whispered. "Has the war come here?"

"No, of course not, it's not possible," said Anya. "The war is over."

"The war is over, the war is over," the children shouted, heaving their snowballs into the air. Erik stood alone in the yard, clutching his notebook, watching Anya's reaction.

"What do you think is happening?" asked Maddie.

"I don't know," Anya said.

Their attention was drawn to the wagon rumbling up the road to the schoolyard.

"It's Mr. Dodge!" said Maddie.

Before the wagon came to a full stop, the old man jumped down, stumbling as he came toward them. His voice was stricken. "The president's been shot!" he gasped. He tossed the reins to Maddie. "Sister, walk her some to cool her down." His eyes were red and haggard. "Only the devil himself would shoot our president on Good Friday."

Anya was stunned to see the farmer so distraught, for he was a stalwart man. The children had frozen in place, silent now, faces blank.

"Is he dead?" she asked.

"He's in the Lord's hands now."

Anya turned away, confused. She had hated the president, holding him responsible for the war and all of the pain it had wrought. Now Abraham Lincoln had been murdered. Many times she had wished him dead, but the reality was shocking to her.

"We will gather in the village after supper, in the church." He took the reins from Maddie and climbed aboard the wagon. In silence they watched the old man depart.

"What should we do now?" asked Maddie.

"I don't know. I guess you should all go home."

There was nothing to go home for, Maddie thought. In the evening, her father and brother sat at the table in silence, barely swallowing the food she'd spent hours to prepare. She tried to cook things her mother had made, hoping that the house would begin to smell like home again, but time and again she made a botch of it. In any case, no one noticed, one way or the other. Charlie was the worst, throwing fits, hiding to worry her, crying at night like a baby, wetting his bed.

"Anya, you could come with us," she said. "You could stay with us tonight, in my room."

"Maddie, not this time." Anya knew she could not join the Grindstone community in mourning for the fallen president. She did not feel as they did, she would not bow her head in grief nor make a mockery of theirs.

She locked the schoolhouse and headed to her cabin. Although the breeze had a bite to it, she could feel the sun on her shoulders. It would be weeks before the wildflowers bloomed, but the path was carpeted with spongy green moss and the air smelled rich with river life. Flocks of geese were on the move, swirling about the sky then settling in the meadow by the bay. Herons and fisher hawks called high above her, and her spirits lifted with them.

She continued down the path to the sheltered cove, where Emil the Frenchman kept his dugout canoe. He wouldn't miss it—a month earlier, he had told Anya that he was heading north to the Laurentians. Too crowded in the islands, he'd said, might as well be living in the City of Montreal. Be gone 'til next winter. He said he had a woman up there, a red Indian wife and a whole family of Indian babies. Looking at his stooped figure, his teeth all but gone, she had doubted this to be the case, but what did she know of such matters?

The bay was calm; had there been any chop to it, Anya would not have dared to take the boat, for she could not swim. The canoe was solid, however, so she pulled off her boots and stockings and tied up her skirt with her shawl. With a push Anya sent the boat into the shallows and climbed aboard. As she pulled away from the shore, her actions were clumsy, the paddle catching every wave, but she took pleasure in her strength. She remembered what it was like to be young.

A handful of islands were scattered below Grindstone, almost identical with their granite outcroppings and fringe of pine. She had no destination in mind. As she paddled, she practiced her strokes, striving to keep them even. After awhile she became winded and stopped, looking around for direction; she had traveled farther from Grindstone than she had intended. Still, the sky was light and the river glassy, so she paused to enjoy the peace. It was then that she heard the sound, so soft at first that she thought it her imagination. Then she heard it again, the sound of a violin, plaintive as a voice.

Anya did not know the refrain, but the music that carried across the water was so filled with longing, such sadness, that she set the paddle in the canoe and closed her eyes. In the gentle rocking of the boat she was carried back to a time that had been lost to her.

It is cealidh night at Dan Mahoney's and they are all together. The music begins with a fiddle or two, and as it takes hold, more join in, with a tin whistle and a drum made of goatskin. Tonight, seven fiddlers are at it, "Finnegan's Reel," stomping the floor with their heavy boots. Michael Byrne is the master. Legend has it that he tunes his fiddle to the song of the nightingale. The Donegal fiddlers have made a name for themselves, their playing fierce and inventive.

After the applause, an old man, a stranger to the village, stands and starts to play. He begins slowly, with a simple phrase turning on itself. It builds and builds all of a piece then lifts to the heavens. But there is no glory in the soaring, it is the saddest music she has ever heard. His eyes are closed and tears roll down his cheeks as he plays.

He is from Connemara and he mourns its countless dead, its empty villages. He is a medium, Anya realizes, anguish flowing through him, and she wonders if he himself is even a mortal man. As she looks around the room she sees tears streaming down the faces of the listeners. Even Finn is moved, though when he feels her eyes upon him, he screws up his face. Anya understands that the fiddler has honored Ireland's lost ones and that he has done a holy thing. After the traveler finishes, the room is silent for a long time, as if in prayer, then one fiddler, then another, jump into a reel, rollicking and naughty, and all is well again.

Their father tells Finn and Anya that the old man is like a trouba-
dour of old who travels the countryside telling Ireland's history through his
music. Anya's mother turns to her, eyes soft, and takes her hand. She is still
pretty, with her dark hair and eyes, and she is wearing the periwinkle-blue
shawl that Anya loves. Anya leans into the curve of her mother's body, ig-
noring Finn. Their da is tapping the table now, though abstractedly, for he
is troubled by the old man's music. Finn will pull him out of it with some
deviltry. He will make a show of swigging his father's ale or hop to his feet
for some fancy step-dancing, and they will laugh again, restored by Finn's
merriment.

Anya was lost in reverie for but a few moments, though deeply
enough so that when she came back to herself, she looked about and did
not recognize at first where she was. Then she shook off her melancholy
and paddled home in the shadow of Grindstone. The war was over, Finn
was surely traveling north by now and would arrive any day. Although it
would soon be dark, she was not afraid. Anya thought about the music,
and the person playing it, and took comfort in the thought that there
was a kindred spirit in these islands so far from home.

CHAPTER 17

THE TOLLING OF BELLS echoed amidst the islands so that they seemed to come at once from heaven and earth. Then the cannons, deafening, infernal, familiar. Douglas had been out on the river, and a fellow fisherman, full of the news, had pulled alongside his skiff. The stranger had approached him with urgency, and as the fisherman's boat drew near, Douglas pulled his hat low, gripping the pistol in his coat pocket.

The man was from downriver, and the news had passed quickly, vessel to vessel, such was its weight. So Booth had finally gone through with it. Lincoln was dead.

When he returned to his hut, he dug through the newspapers and found the image of Grant and Lee taken at Appomattox just a few days earlier, when the treaty had been signed. Lee, dignified to the end, looking worn, older than he remembered. An honorable man, like his father, troubled by the concept of slavery but loyal to his homeland. They had the stuff of Greek kings. At least Grant had accorded Lee some measure of dignity in his surrender. Now Johnson would take Lincoln's place. Lincoln had been wrong, tragically so, but he'd been a decent man. Now his sot of a vice president was demanding that Lee be hanged for a traitor.

The newspapers would run Booth's portrait for weeks – good for trade. They would fuel the fire, for inevitably there would be talk of conspiracy and retribution. It was hard to imagine how much more punishment the South could endure. Richmond had already been devastated, and with every report the details were more terrible. In the vortex of war, the city had been sacked by its own, even before the Federals arrived, the elegant buildings burned to rubble, the streets filled with filth. Its own arsenal had caught fire, launching shells against itself, ten thousand of them, a vision as grotesque as anything Dante had conjured.

Had the house been destroyed? He imagined the smashed piano, the heavy drapes lifting flames to the second floor, the graceful windows exploding in the heat. The gardens which should now be in full bloom—his mother's cherished heirloom roses, Empress Josephine and Charles the First. Was all of it gone? The newspapers had described the women of Richmond, dressed in mourning, climbing about their homes like wraiths or madwomen, searching for the remains of their former lives. Were his mother and sister among them?

He pulled his violin from beneath his pallet and left the cabin, heading for the rise that faced north. He knew he was taking a risk. The church bells had ceased, and on such a quiet evening the sound would carry for miles. Yet he could not stop himself. As the sun began to set he realized that it was Passover.

When he played, he usually became lost in the music itself, the logic of the progressions, the discipline of Mozart's vision. This evening, however, he remembered his family gathered together for the Seder, his mother and father, his sister, Sara. Jakob, the youngest, reciting the Four Questions.

Why is this night different from all other nights, from all other nights?

Jakob had been lucky; his body buried within a few hours by his comrades, not left to rot in the field by his enemies. Many of the corpses he had seen were unrecognizable even as human beings. Many of those who had survived the battlefield could not be saved: there was a special place in hell for Monsieur Minie, who had devised a bullet that inflicted such irreparable damage. The long nights of surgery at the field hospitals, men stacked outside on litters, deranged, crying out or oblivious with shock. He took such pains with them – each soldier could well have been his brother – and he knew that as skillful has he had become, many would be dead in a few days, not from surgery but from fever. His skills were of little help to those boys who died anyway, of sepsis or inflammation of the brain. He felt helpless, they all did, because no one knew where the fever came from and how to prevent it.

Jakob had made an excellent soldier. He had devoted himself to his calling, he had wanted to make his father proud. Proud? Their father had been dead for years. His heart had simply stopped one night in his sleep, when his older son was studying medicine in Baltimore, the younger one still a boy. At that time his grief for his father had been so profound that he could not imagine anything worse happening to him in his lifetime. Now, in the face of all else that had happened, his father's death seemed untimely but not essentially tragic.

Still, he sorely missed his father and often found himself engaged in conversation with him, at least in his mind. Even so, he knew that for all of his father's experience, he could not have guided his sons through these hard times. His father's medical experience would be useless against the wounds he himself had encountered, his ethical standards seriously compromised by the very nature of this war. Douglas tried to imagine a dialogue with his father in which he would explain why he had joined the conspiracy and why, in the end, he had betrayed his own comrades.

He closed his eyes and began to chant the psalm for the dead for his brother Jakob. *El malei rachamim, shochayn bam'romim, ham-tzay m'nucha n'chona al kanfay Hash'china.* Then he picked up his violin and began to play.

CHAPTER 18

KENNEDY ASSEMBLED THE GROUP in Toronto in the anteroom of the cathedral of St. Lawrence. Four loyal members of the Knights of the Golden Circle: Campbell, O'Leary, Ramsey, and Blunt. He knew three of them only by reputation. Only Blunt had taken part in the New York conspiracy, and he'd had a minor role; their target would not recognize them. Jacob Thompson had since headed back to Mississippi. He wanted no part of this search, for he still could not believe in the guilt of his old friend's son. Nor did he want anything to do with the Knights.

"The KGC are scoundrels," he said. "Terrorizing innocent blacks and decent Southerners under the guise of Confederate pride. They taint our good name."

Kennedy did not share Thompson's daintiness. The loyalists' ruthlessness would serve his needs and then he would be rid of them. He'd dealt with such men before.

Construction on the cathedral was still in progress, and workmen made their way up and down the aisles carrying buckets of plaster.

"Never mind them," said Kennedy. "They'll think we're wanting a place to cool ourselves."

"Cool? Me clackers are freezin' in here," said O'Leary.

"What do we know?" asked Campbell.

Kennedy circulated the sketch. "He's tall, close to six feet. Dark eyes, dark hair. Scar on his brow. Twenty-five at most. Educated, a surgeon before and during the war. A Jew."

Blunt snorted. "Loyal only to their own kind. Only thing Grant was right about."

Kennedy frowned. "Don't assume anything—he fought at Gettysburg and Chancellorsville. Think about the details that might catch him up."

"Family?"

"Genteel. A mother and sister in Richmond, father dead, brother killed at Gettysburg. Didn't gamble, go with whores, even the refined ones. Plays the violin, carries it with him all the time." After a moment he continued. "Smart, not one to freeze up in battle, that's why Thompson chose him."

He pulled a packet from his pocketbook and dispersed funds to the men. "Fan out, work in pairs. Look in the mill houses, taverns, boat works. It's unlikely he'll be in this area, but we'll pick up clues as to which direction he headed. I don't want to waste time in Detroit if he's already in Kingston, heading to Nova Scotia. We'll meet here tomorrow at sunset."

The men dispersed. Kennedy walked up the main thoroughfare to the hotel where Thomson and McDonald had called them together, when there was still hope that the Confederacy would triumph, and Robbie was still alive.

CHAPTER 19

FOR WEEKS THE ASSASSINATION was all anyone spoke of. At the farmers' market, walking home from the lumber mill, the men argued about the conspiracy, their voices ringing in anger. The boys who had been too young to enlist followed in their wake, burning with youth-fever to fight. At Brady's Mercantile one could hardly find space to stand. Many like Brady had lost a loved one to the war, and sentiments were strong. Lincoln was now a martyr, a saint.

His replacement, all agreed, was a disaster. "Johnson is a scoundrel and a shite, a man who was drunk at his own inauguration." Brady threw a log into the stove, jabbing it with a poker, wrenching the door closed. "He wants only vengeance, he who lost nothing in the war. Now it will never be over."

The papers stirred the pot, describing the desperate actions of the assassin, the infamous John Wilkes Booth. Anya had seen his portrait and thought him handsome, dashing as well as desperate. It was surely the stuff of drama, his leaping to the stage and shouting "*Sic Semper Tyrannis!*" – Thus Always to Tyrants! – as if he were in a play by William Shakespeare. A writer could not have invented a more astonishing character, and perhaps that was what Booth had become, in his own mind, a leading figure in some great drama. He certainly was to his audience, which, according to the newspapers, was now worldwide.

Booth had been captured in a matter of days, but the search for his accomplices took on a life of its own. One of Booth's collaborators was rumored to be hiding out in the islands of the St. Lawrence. People saw him everywhere, even on Grindstone. A number of hapless tinkers and travelers were rounded up for questioning, and worse. In such a climate, gossip became fact, evidence enough to condemn a man. Anya had seen it happen in Kilcar: reprisals generated by rumors, half-heard conversations, a suspicious-looking countenance. Innocence became irrelevant when it was all for the greater cause. And there were those, of course, who simply loved the thrill of the hunt.

It was the custom on Grindstone to celebrate Mid-Summer's Eve, a tradition brought by the Swedes. In late June, the river shimmered like blue silk, and daylight lingered well past nine with a clarity that seemed otherworldly. Then, as darkness settled, the trees and meadows were lit with fireflies. Anya had never seen them before, an insect, plainer than a beetle, casting such a spell on the world. The magic was short-lived, and perhaps therein lay its power.

Maddie had pressed Anya to take her and Charlie to the festival. "With school closed, I don't see you anymore. And if you don't come, we can't go," she added, her voice aggrieved. "Father's still sad, and Michael…" She made a face.

Anya laughed. "I can hardly say no, can I?"

Together they baked three fruit pies for the occasion, carefully packing them in a hamper. To Maddie's annoyance, Charlie kept opening the basket and looking at them. It was nice to hear the children bickering, Anya thought. They were obviously excited by the event and were beginning to set their grief aside.

It was a glorious afternoon, the fields bright with buttercups, as lovely as any meadow in Ireland. They could hear the musicians before the wagon crested the hill, and Charlie began to bounce excitedly. Maddie turned to Anya, clapping her hands. "I know that song! I bet it's Mac Drummond playing! He's very good."

From the rise, they could see men and women crowding around tables, children darting from the periphery to grab some treat. Mac Drummond was, indeed, fiddling, accompanied by a man with a whistle and another with a goatskin drum. The tables were laden with early summer fare and Maddie placed their offerings on the table as if they were blessed.

Anya was enjoying herself, led about by Charlie, sampling this and that from the platters on the tables. Wild strawberries, as sweet as spring itself, and dandelion greens and rhubarb. Sweet cream and scones, the recipes from Scotland. Raspberries would come later, she was told, prized for their ephemeral nature, then huckleberries, if the bears left any behind. When Anya first came to America, such bounty had troubled her. She had resented the robust health of these people, the rounded arms and plump cheeks of the children who knew nothing of want. In those days, she could eat little; her senses were too acute and she was easily sickened. Now she saw things differently. Anya had learned how hard it was to manage a farm, and that during the war the burden had fallen onto the shoulders of the women and children, and the men too old to fight. The bountiful table was the fruit of their honest labors. The islanders would see it as a gift from God meant to be shared.

After a moment, Anya noticed that Erik Karlson was standing near her, as if summoning the courage to speak with her. The boy blushed and it took a few moments for him to compose himself.

"How nice to see you, Erik!"

He produced from his overalls a folded packet. Silently he handed it to her. Anya smiled at him and unfolded the butcher paper. On the back the boy had sketched the flowers of early spring.

"How lovely these are!" The drawings were delicate, accurate.

"These are mayflowers, M'am. They're blue. But I didn't have any colors."

"But they are wonderful as they are. You are very talented."

"It's for you," he mumbled, ducking his head. "For your cabin." With that, he ran off. Anya carefully rolled up the drawing and tucked it into their food basket under the table.

"Mrs. MacGregor?" Meg Robinson stood before her, smiling and twisting her hands. Meg was too old for schooling, and Anya knew her only because she sometimes stopped by the schoolhouse to walk her little sister home. Meg looked very pretty, her blonde hair curling about her face, the blue of her gown matching her eyes. "I saw that you came with the Burns children. It was sad about their mother."

Anya nodded, scanning the crowd for Charlie's bright red hair.

"Michael avoids me, Mrs. MacGregor."

Anya turned to the lass, surprised. In all her months on Grindstone, she's spoken to Meg only a few times.

"We...we made promises when he left for the war."

Anya didn't know what to say.

"When Michael came back, I was there at the landing. But I might have been invisible, for all he saw. Or just an acquaintance. I under-stood, because of the hospital and all. He wasn't himself." Her face was flushed with emotion. "When I finally went to the farm to see him, he sent Maddie to tell me to go away, that he was ill!" Her eyes filled with tears. "Why? Do you think it's because of his leg? I don't care! I've known him all my life! Nothing's changed."

Anya looked at her. How could it not matter to Michael that his lower left leg had been blown off? Nothing would remind him of his loss more than this vibrant, healthy girl who had known him when he was whole. For him everything had changed. She remembered one morning at the farm when she'd come down to start the breakfast fire and saw Michael looking about his own kitchen as if he did not know where he was.

"He and his friends, they're moving about like a pack of school-boys." Meg's voice was filled with aggrievement.

"Michael's here?"

"They're out behind the church. I believe they've brought whisky."

Anya knew that Maddie would be upset when she realized that Michael had come on his own, without telling her, so excusing herself, Anya looked about for Maddie and Charlie, finding them at the food table, sampling everything in sight. "Let's watch the dancers," she said, taking their hands.

A group of lads had gathered around the planked floor, boisterous, stomping and hooting to the music. A few men stepped-danced, nimble, leaping high into the air. Maddie laughed with delight at their antics, clapping loudly, and Charlie mimicked them. Then the fiddlers slipped into a reel and the dancing began in earnest. The music caught Anya as well, and she could not keep still, clapping and stamping her feet. There were not enough men for partners, and so the women danced with one another. Anya and Maddie clasped hands, romping through the reels.

Michael and his friends rejoined the group of onlookers. He watched Anya and his sister whooping around the floor and found himself smiling. Maddie looked again like the child she was, laughing aloud, swinging wildly out of step with the music. Anya was twirling about, showing Maddie and Charlie some fancy steps. She looked up and saw him watching her, and stopped. Then she gave him a friendly smile, and he nodded in return, then moved away.

Anya felt a tugging on her arm and turned around to see Charlie. "Anya." He looked tired and grubby, ready for bed.

"It's time to go home," she said. She picked him up and carried him to the wagon. "Wait here, Charlie. Stay put." The boy was already half-asleep. She found Maddie standing by the barn, listening to Michael and his friends. Their voices had become heated.

"Booth was in Toronto last winter, that's where the plans were set."

"You know they're in the islands. Don't you read the papers?"

"Never learned how."

"I saw someone yesterday at the creamery. Soon as I rode up, he disappeared into the woods like a bit of smoke, smooth as you please."

"Did you get a look at him?"

"Wasn't an islander. He was on foot, that's why I noticed. Didn't want to be seen. Didn't have my sidearm with me, otherwise I would have followed him."

"Bastards, shooting the president in the head."

"From behind! The act of a base coward."

"They were all cowards, filthy Rebs."

Then Michael spoke. "You're full of shite. The Rebs we fought were as brave as we were."

The men went silent.

"Could be just a deserter."

"There's gold stashed on one of the islands. Blood money for Lincoln's murderers."

With that Anya took Maddie's hand and hurried to their wagon. Maddie drove back to the farm, Anya beside her, Charlie sleeping soundly in the back of the wagon. Maddie and Anya were silent, lost in their own thoughts, and only Charlie's contented snoring bespoke the good times that they'd had earlier that evening. Anya closed her eyes, lulled by the jostle of the wagon. She thought about Meg Robinson and her hopes for the future and tried to imagine her and Michael's wedding, Meg in a fancy gown, Michael in a frock coat standing before the minister. It would never happen. Meg would have to make peace with her past and move on. She was young and pretty and would doubtless find another. Anya was realistic about her own chances for a family. She would make a life as a schoolmistress and a home for her brother when he returned. It would be enough.

CHAPTER 20

A FEW WEEKS LATER, Michael Burns appeared at her cabin. Anya was hacking with a hoe at the weeds in her kitchen garden. When she heard his horse, she looked up, wiping her hands on her apron. "What's wrong?" she called. "Is something wrong at home?"

He walked the horse into the yard. "The 94th is coming back today. Coming in on the train."

"Michael! Are you going to Clayton? Please, take me with you!"

"That's why I'm here. Ferry's leaving soon, better hurry."

She pulled off her apron and ran back into the cabin. A few moments later she emerged in a clean blouse, smoothing her hair, giddy with excitement. He'd never seen her like this and hoped he hadn't made a mistake. He didn't want to be responsible for what they would encounter at the train station, if her husband would even be there or bear any resemblance to the man she remembered.

As she walked towards him, however, he saw that she was more anxious than excited. She had waited for so long that it now seemed almost too much to bear. Michael pulled her up behind him, and they set off at a trot for the landing.

Clayton was decked for the holiday, the buildings draped with bunting, the streets crowded with townspeople and islanders milling about, chatting excitedly, shouting to one another as they made their way to the station. There Anya saw Seamus Brady, waving, smiling broadly as if he were the village mayor. The regiment had done themselves proud, Michael thought, chasing Lee all the way to Appomattox. How he wished he'd been there at the Courthouse with his mates. It might have made up for some of the rest.

Even without his crutches he moved haltingly in the crowd. "If you want to go ahead, I don't mind," he said.

"No, Michael," she said. "We came together." She took his arm and they walked together in what had become a procession of hundreds of people.

A band of musicians had gathered to play. Anya watched the man with the fiddle, whose face was ravaged on one side by burns. He'd lost an eye and an ear and his hair grew in tufts around the scars on his scalp. Suddenly chilled, she moved closer to Michael as they made their way onto the platform.

They heard the train from some distance, and small boys began leaping across the tracks, back and forth, with excitement. Then it rounded the bend, spewing great clouds of steam, clattering, creaking to a halt. The crowd let out a roar and began frantically to wave. Michael did not mind that Anya was now gripping his arm like a vise. She seemed to need all the support she could find.

Men leaned out of the windows, waving and calling, and the train was mobbed. Then the crowd broke away as the veterans climbed down the steps, blinking in the sun, as if they had been indoors for a long time. Some were damaged, some were sound. Michael strained to see each face. Then he saw a comrade and, tears filling his eyes, shouted his name. He pushed into the surging crowd and disappeared. Anya stayed where she was, twisting the ends of her shawl. Every now and then she would spot a soldier who resembled Finn in height or color of hair, and her heart would catch, but then she would see that she had been mistaken. Finally all of the able-bodied men had disembarked. Then a soldier whose eyes were bandaged slowly felt his way down the steps, led by a comrade. Several more were lifted from the train in stretchers, then set down on the platform amid the waiting families.

When no one else came down the steps, Anya moved through the crowd, thinking she must have missed him, peering into this face, the next. Then she boarded the train. She ran though the car, then the next one, catching her gown on the one of the seats.

A soldier was moving down the aisle. "Miss! What are you doing?"

"Are there no more?"

His voice was kind. "No more."

Anya looked beyond him as if she didn't believe him. "But my brother should be here."

"There are no more on the train."

"Finn MacGregor."

He shook his head.

"Would he have gotten off at another station?"

"The captain's on the platform. He'll have a list."

The officer was mobbed by men and women as desperate as she was to find their loved ones. She could not contain herself, cutting in front of the rest. "My brother should have been on this train. MacGregor." She spelled it for him. "Finn MacGregor."

He scanned the list then looked at her. "Finn O'Neill MacGregor?"

"Yes!"

"He's in prison," the man said. "Desertion."

Anya felt as if she'd been punched. "What prison?"

"Capitol Prison, Washington," he read. "Twenty-fourth Day of December, 1864."

Anya turned away, pushing through the crowd. She was struggling to get air, there was not enough air to breathe. Then she spotted Seamus Brady heading down the path to his store. She caught up with him as he was unlocking the door. Before she could stop them, tears began to course down her cheeks. Aghast, Brady took her arm. "Come inside."

She told him what she had heard. "Mr. Brady, would they truly put Finn in prison after he was wounded in battle?"

"Aye, they'd pull Christ from the cross and His mother too if they had the chance. The bloody bastards."

"What does it mean?"

That it's likely he's been hanged and stuffed into an unmarked grave, Brady thought. "We'll contact them," he said. "We'll find someone to bribe. We'll find out if he's still in prison."

"I'll leave today," she said. "I have money."

He exhaled loudly. "Mrs. MacGregor. He may not be there, he may have been transferred to a prison in the North. Look, I'll see what I can find out." He paused. "You can't go down there, not until you know if there's any point."

"How long would it take?"

"A week, no more than that." He watched as she struggled with the idea. If she had her way, he knew she would climb aboard the next train to New York, get herself robbed before she got to Philadelphia.

"I can't wait a week. He's already been there too long."

He handed her a sheet of paper. "Write it all down. I'll go to the telegraph office this afternoon. Man owes me a favor. Come back in seven days."

"Four. No more."

"You drive a hard bargain, Mrs. MacGregor." He smiled but she had already turned away. He watched her leave the store then folded the note and tucked it in his ledger. The lass had no sense at all of the size of this country. Well, he would find someone who knew someone, call in some debts. If the lad had been hanged, he'd contrive some story, help her get used to the idea.

As Anya walked to the ferry, she saw that the crowd had begun to disperse. The weather had turned foul, the rain driven by a cold north wind. The bunting hung in tatters, and wet festoons and garlands clogged the puddles on Water Street. Anya's hair and clothing were soaked and halfway across the channel she was shivering with cold. It wasn't until they landed that Anya realized she had forgotten all about Michael Burns. He would be with his comrades; surely he hadn't wasted time looking for her. Tears stung her eyes when she remembered the look on his face when he'd spotted his friend.

Emmet Dodge was not at the landing to meet the travelers, so she hiked to her cabin in the downpour, sidestepping the rivulets that ran down the road. Her skirts were sopping, dragging against her legs, her boots filled with water. Finn had been in prison since Christmas Eve, a death sentence hanging over him. All those months she had been going about her business, safe and warm. She'd even been happy. Would they put him before a firing squad or would he be hanged?

She saw Finn standing above her on a scaffold made of rough timbers. He was thin, ragged, his hands tied behind his back. An old priest stood next to him, urging him to pray. Finn looked down at her, his face pale, his dark eyes somber, resigned.

By the time Anya got to the cabin, she was frantic. She'd had enough of waiting, she would go to Washington herself the very next day. She dropped her satchel on the porch and ran to the edge of the woods where she had buried Finn's money. The ground was soggy and she worried that the hole had filled with water, destroying the bank notes. She dropped to her knees and, hands shaking, scraped away the debris she had piled on top of it, pulling away the stone. Water was seeping into the hole, but there was the tobacco tin, as she'd hid it months earlier. It left rust on her hands, but the lid was intact.

"Annie?"

She was so startled that she dropped the tin, and it rolled away from her under some ferns. Jonathon Douglas stood above her. Even in the downpour, water streaming from his broad-brimmed hat, she recognized him immediately. She felt for the tin until she found it, and clutching it in her hands, turned to face him, tears coursing down her face.

DONNA WALSH INGLEHART

CHAPTER 21

SHE STRUGGLED TO HER FEET, ignoring the hand that he held out to her. Her clothing was saturated, her hair plastered to her cheeks, and he saw that the color had drained from her face, her lips turning blue. It was obvious that she had gotten badly chilled. He pulled her onto the porch.

"Annie, let's get out of the rain." He could feel her body trembling against his, so hard that he finally lifted her and carried her into the cabin, closing the door against the rain.

Once inside, he set her down and pulled off her soaked boots and stockings, then went about building a fire. He struck a match to the birch bark and in a few moments, the fire was roaring. When he turned around, she was still standing there, shivering, clenched against the cold. Water dripping from her gown pooled at her feet.

He went to her trunk, and rummaging through her clothing found a flannel nightdress. "Annie, you must put this on. You've caught a chill."

She looked at him then, her eyes lifeless.

"Come on," he coaxed. When she didn't respond, he began to undo the top buttons of her gown.

At his touch she pulled away from him. "I can do it," she said.

He went out onto the porch. It was still raining hard, the wind blowing in from the north, waves crashing against the shore. By the time he returned with a load of wood, she had changed into her night-gown, her soaked skirt dripping from a hook by the fireplace. Her hair hung in wet ropes around her shoulders. He found a bit of linen and toweled her hair, then gently dried her face, her neck and hands, as if she were a child. He pulled a blanket from the bed and wrapping it around her, settled her before the hearth. He then hung his jacket and hat on a hook and sat down on the rug beside her.

"Annie, what happened?"

As tears filled her eyes, she roughly wiped them away. "He wasn't on the train."

"The regiment returned?"

"He's in prison for desertion."

He felt the anger course through him. He'd seen too many men become bewildered by the war, good men who had fought bravely, who had seen and been ordered to do unimaginable things. Her brother had been wounded once, no one should blame him for wanting out of it. "What prison?"

"Capitol."

"I know the place."

She turned to him, her voice urgent. "Please help me, Jonathon. You must know someone I could bribe. I have three hundred dollars."

"The conscription fee."

"Aye, I've not touched a penny. How long will it take me to get to Washington?"

"Annie, it would be better for you to hire a detective."

Her voice was angry. "I can't sit here and do nothing."

He stood and went to his jacket and pulled a flask from his pocket. "Here," he said, unscrewing the top. "This will calm your nerves."

She took a sip, coughed, then took another.

"That's enough," he said. He took the flask from her then drank from it himself.

"Finn isn't my husband, he's my twin." Her voice was thick with tears. "My parents are dead, and my baby sister Aisling. He's all I have left."

He took her hand. It felt small in his, cold. He began to massage it, gently, then the other one. Her pulse was steadier and her face had more color. "We'll get him out. There's always someone to bribe. And Capitol Prison has no security at all, it's notorious for escapes."

"Seamus Brady promised to wire someone today, he said he would know in four days."

"Can you trust the man?"

"Aye. He's been kind to me."

"Then you should wait until you hear something. He will be able to arrange a bribe."

She nodded. He drew her close, wrapping his arms around her, and she leaned against him. The fire crackled and snapped, throwing shadows onto the ceiling. The rain fell steadily, softly, pattering against the roof. Soon the owl began to call, and then the loons.

After awhile Anya spoke, her voice so low he could hardly hear her. "They frightened me so, when I first came here. They sounded like banshees! Then I saw how beautiful they were, how devoted to their mates and their chicks."

"This reminds me of a place where I used to go," he said, "a hunting camp up in the mountains, where my father brought my brother and me from the time we were boys. We would go for a few weeks in the fall, in November, when there was a bit of snow on the ground, and bring back a couple of turkeys, maybe a deer." He took another swig from the flask. "It was a long time ago."

"What is your brother's name?"

"Jakob."

She looked at him. "It was you who stayed here last winter, it was your book I found, the Keats. I should have known it."

"It was. I was caught in a blizzard. I'm sorry."

"It doesn't matter." She stood and went to the shelf and retrieved it. She passed it to him and settled again before the fire. He opened the book and looked at the inscription, then closed it again. "Thank you," he said finally.

"Jonathon, where is your brother?"

It was harder than he thought to say the words aloud. "He was killed at Gettysburg."

She turned to him, and in the firelight, her eyes were filled with sorrow. Instinctively she reached toward him and touched his face. She smoothed his hair, then closed her eyes and kissed him on the forehead then his lips.

Her hair smelled of lavender and sweet grass, the river. He wrapped it around his fingers and closed his eyes, inhaling its scent, then pulled her to him, kissing her gently at first, then more urgently. She moved away from him, then looking at him all the while, slipped off her night-gown, her dark hair about her shoulders, her skin as pale as moonlight. Putting her arms around his neck, she pulled him to her. And her breath on his face, his heart beating hard, he drove away the years of death.

As the fire turned to embers and the room grew chill, they moved to the narrow bed, and he drew the quilt over them both. She sighed then murmured a few indistinguishable words. After a moment, she began to breathe more rhythmically. She had fallen asleep. He felt such tender-ness toward her, a protectiveness that surprised him. Annie, this Irish girl from a whitewashed village by the sea. For all their differences, they shared a kinship, adrift as they were in this strange land.

He shifted onto his side, and as she began to stir, he kissed her on her neck then her breasts. She was fully awake now, and in the moon-light he saw again how beautiful she was. Shy in her nakedness, she looked at him uncertainly, tugging the blanket to cover herself. He pulled it aside and moved on top of her and again they become one, as if it had always been so.

When was the last time he had held a woman in his arms, the last time he had felt something like desire? He had thought himself dead for so long. He chose this girl instead.

As dawn broke, she traced his brow, the scar on his chest, imagining that she knew everything there was to know about him. He touched her as if he knew her as well, as if he had known her all his life.

He turned her hand over, rubbing his fingers gently along the groove in her palm. "How did you get this scar? And these burns?"

"After Finn left, I was on my own. The burns are from lye, from a laundry." She frowned. "The cut –."

"What happened?"

She shrugged. He kissed her palm and then the star-like pattern of scars.

"I pretend it is a sign of my bond with the merrows."

"The merrows?"

"Silkies, women of the sea. Sometimes a man catches one, with love or deception, and she will stay with him awhile on land. But she always longs for her true home and always returns."

He looped a strand of her hair around his fingers. "Is that how you feel?"

"I don't know where my true home is. Everything in Ireland is lost." She was silent for awhile. "I miss the sea. Where we lived in Kilcar, the sound was always there, like a heartbeat. When Finn and I crossed into America from Kingston, I thought the lake was like the ocean, and so it would feel like home. But it unnerved me, it didn't smell like the sea— no dolphins or whales. It seemed like a great barren space, even though they hauled out fish by the boatloads."

"It's only what you are used to. It is beautiful here, in its way." As he said it, he realized it was true. "Say your name for me in Irish."

Then he repeated it, *Áine*, catching the sounds. She taught him some phrases in Gaelic, some naughty ones learned from Finn, and laughed to hear them coming from him, his accent was so accurate. It was the first time he had heard her laugh, he realized. It was a remarkable sound.

Then she taught him some tender words so that she could hear him say the phrases to her in Irish. "*A rún*," she said. My secret love.

"*A rún*," he replied. "What does it mean?"

When she would not tell him, he laughed aloud and enfolded her in his arms. Soon he was fast asleep.

131

For awhile, Anya's grief fell away from her. At his touch, in his gaze, she had become lovely and young, and all things seemed possible. Finn was alive and the world was whole again, the fractures healed.

CHAPTER 22

HE WOKE WITH A START, awakening her from her reverie. "Someone's outside," he whispered.

Then she, too, heard the sound of hooves on the bridge as a horse approached the cabin. He climbed out of bed then pulled a pistol from his jacket. Moving to the window, he peered through the break in the curtains. Then he signaled Anya to look for herself.

Michael Burns was sitting his horse, surveying the yard. Then he looked toward the cabin and brought his horse forward, as if he would dismount.

"It's just Michael, a friend from a neighboring farm. We went to Clayton yesterday to meet the train—he must be wondering why I left him." She realized how odd it would seem to Michael that she was still abed. She pulled on her gown, hurriedly buttoning the bodice.

He lifted the gun, cocking it, and aimed it at Michael.

Horrified, she gripped his arm. "What are you doing?"

Without taking his eyes off Michael, he shrugged her loose.

"But he's harmless!" she whispered angrily. She hurried to the door, and unbolting the latch, stepped onto the porch, then pulled the door shut behind her.

"Good morning!" she called, resisting the urge to smooth her dress. She suddenly felt indecent, with her hair hanging down her shoulders like a slattern, and so she looped the strands in a knot.

Michael looked at her and then at the cabin. "Is everything all right, Mrs. MacGregor? I looked for you yesterday, I didn't see you. Has your husband returned?"

"No, he was not on the train. I'm sorry I left without you, Michael. I hope you didn't wait for me."

"Did they have any news of him?"

There was too much to explain. "No, nothing."

He looked again at the house and then at her. "I'm sorry for that."

"Thank you, Michael. Thank you for stopping by." Please leave, she thought, please leave now.

He loosened the reins and turned about as if to depart, then paused. "Charlie wanted me to ask you when you would come to see him at the farm. Maddie would have said the same but she's too proud to ask."

"I'll come soon. Tell them soon." She hoped that Michael did not hear the urgency in her voice. She stood in the yard, arms folded, as he rode up the lane to the bridge, listening for the clatter of hooves on wood as he picked up speed.

Then she stepped back into the cabin and closed the door. Leaning against it, she looked at the man standing by the window. His expression was altered, his body tense. He looked older, guarded, and when he turned to her she thought he had forgotten who she was.

"He's gone," she said finally.

After a moment he uncocked the pistol.

"Jonathon, he's gone," she repeated, staring at him in disbelief. "What is it? Are you a deserter?"

"I am."

"How long?"

"Since Cold Harbor." He sat on the bed and began to pull on his boots. "I'm sorry, Annie."

She watched him in silence.

He stood and pulled his braces over his shoulders, tucking in his shirt. "I should not have come to you." His voice was weary. "I am not a free man. I had no right to bring this upon you."

She felt anger begin to build within her. "Bring what upon me?"

He made no move to touch her. "Anya, you must tell no one that

I've been here. No one. You know nothing about me."

"I don't know anything about you. Was anything you told me true?"

He looked at her. "You know what was true. What we felt was true." He pulled his hat from the rack. "Promise me, Annie. You must tell no one."

She watched him in silence.

"When it is safe to do so, I will come back," he said. Then he left, latching the door behind himself.

She looked around the cabin, at the disheveled bedclothes, the shirt and trousers on the floor. Her bed was still warm, and now he was gone.

She climbed back under the covers and pulled the blankets to her shoulders. She could hardly make sense of what had happened. Why had he come to her?

When he had touched her, she had not been afraid, and it had been the most natural thing in the world to lay with him. Now she felt connected to him in a way she had not imagined possible with anyone, more than if they were betrothed. Surely he must have felt the same connection. She had seen the desire in his eyes.

Desire.

What a fool she had been! He had come to her knowing she was lonely—surely an island girl with an empty bed would welcome some company! He had taken advantage of her. Even in her anger, she knew the thought unworthy. She had been aroused by his tenderness, his desire, she had wanted him in that way. She wanted to be with him again.

She threw off the bedclothes and hurried down to the cove, pulling off her gown. She waded into the water, submerging herself, and then scrubbed herself as if in atonement. Was it possible that she could get a child from one night's lovemaking? She knew a bit about such things; her mother had not been reticent about matters of the female body.

When she finally climbed out, she was chilled and roughly wiped herself dry with her gown.

By then, morning had all but departed, and she set about removing all traces of him from her cabin. She stripped off the bedclothes and slung the quilt over the line then dragged the pallet out into the sun for an airing. Then she swept the hearth and tidied her table, arranging her two chipped cups and plates.

She thought about how he'd looked standing by the window, pistol turned on Michael. She understood that she did not know Jonathon Douglas at all, perhaps she did not even know his real name. He'd come back when it was safe? His words meant nothing. She went outside and searched until she found the tin, and located another hiding place near the woodpile. She would not dwell on what had happened between them, on what would not be.

<hr>

As he rowed back to Maple, he tried to rationalize what he had done. He understood that the seductive weather had lulled him into a dangerous complacency. He had taken to fishing late into the evening, as any free man would. He had stopped, on occasion, at the island creamery to purchase food. How long had it been since he had enjoyed such simple pleasures, sitting in the sun, eating a bit of coarse bread and cheese?

It had seemed reasonable enough, by such logic, to stop by Annie MacGregor's cabin to say goodbye before he left the islands. She was the only person, in all these months, who had become real to him. The truth was, he had gone to her knowing he had nothing to offer her, that they had no future together. In doing so he had treated her like a whore.

Although Annie had given herself freely, passionately, she had been a virgin. In her situation, she might have few enough opportunities for marriage; in his selfishness, had he denied her that possibility? Worse, had he fitted her for whoredom?

During the war prostitutes had followed the camps in tinkers' wagons, as if they were selling tin pans and shovels. Many were immigrants barely out of childhood, and more than a few were war widows who had lost all decent means of support. They often carried disease; he'd warned countless soldiers against the outcome of a weekend's leave. Before the war he'd given little thought to them. "A necessity and a nuisance," that was how his enlightened professor had described them. Not a moral scourge, Franklin had chuckled, just a nuisance, a medical problem. Now Douglas knew that many women in such desperate straits would not live to see their thirties.

He tried to recall his betrothed, Rebekka, but could only summon images of a pretty girl with soft brown curls, his sister's best friend. It had been assumed by both families that he and Rebekka would wed when he completed his studies.

He remembered a summer evening at her country house near Richmond; Jakob and their sister Sara were there, the four of them, laughing, talking late into the night until they heard the carriages depart, running in the damp grass back to the house before their absence was discovered. Running through the kitchen where the house slaves were cleaning up after the party.

Rebekka's family preferred to call them "servants." It had troubled his father, for he had believed that Jews should not own slaves, that it ran against the deepest tenets of his faith. Yet there were rabbis in Richmond who preached that according to the Torah holding slaves was legal and proper. Was Bekka still waiting for him? It was unlikely. It had been more than three years since they had said goodbye. He did not remember their leave-taking. Undoubtedly Bekka had shed tears and had held him close, telling him how brave he was, how proud she was, that she would wait for him forever. Undoubtedly he had pledged that he would be true to her, that he would return to her at the war's end. In no time, they had said. In no time at all the war would be over.

When he got to his camp, he would pack his belongings and ready himself for departure, but now he did not know where he was heading. All he could think about was the desperate nature of Annie's situation. Her store of food was pitiful, even in summer, and while she was not starving, she could not thrive under such circumstances. Her pale complexion was likely the result of anemia.

When he reached Maple Island, he drifted down to the cove and climbed out of the dinghy. He pulled it into the alders where he was sure the boat could not be spotted from the water. This afternoon he would check the progress of the skiff, and while he was in Clayton, buy a Union jacket from someone on the docks. Such a coat would make him anonymous; with so many veterans back from the war, he would not warrant a second glance. He remembered the battlefields, the soldiers myriad and indistinct, their humanity all but lost in the sea of bloody blue and grey uniforms.

While he was in Clayton, he would leave money for Annie with Brady, he would write a letter making it clear that he would never return to these islands, he would never see her again. He would not have her wait for him as she waited for her brother.

When he had lain with her, it was as if he had walked away from it all, as if he had been returned to something of himself. No wonder he had wanted to wrap the girl around himself, to live within the warmth of her body. But through his own weakness, he had pulled Annie into his world. When he was with her, he lost all perspective. He forgot his circumstances, the very real peril of his situation. If Kennedy were to learn of their connection, he would consider Anya an accomplice, equally guilty, and would condemn and punish her without mercy, as an act of war.

CHAPTER 23

BRADY'S STORE WAS SO CROWDED that Anya had to wait on the porch until she could enter. Now that the war was over, shipments had started to move again, and people scrambled for goods they'd done without for years. Brady noted Anya's entrance with a friendly wave, but he was busy with customers and so she fidgeted impatiently until he was free. Finally she could wait no longer and edged her way to the counter.

"Mr. Brady, it's been four day. Have you any news?"

He smiled. "Aye, lass, I do, just as I promised." He pulled from his vest a scrap of paper and read it to her. "'Finn MacGregor is no longer in Capitol Prison. He escaped on the 27th day of March. Whereabouts unknown.'"

Anya stared at him. "Then why was he on the Union list less than a week ago?"

Brady shrugged. "That's the official story. They don't want us to know how many veterans have gone missing."

"Where could he be?"

"Could be anywhere. Very likely he's waiting until people have forgotten he exists. Might have gone out west for awhile. So much to be done after the war, no one will care for long about an Irish lad who's gone missing." He smiled. "Except for you!"

She gripped his hands so tightly that he laughed aloud. "Seamus Brady, swear to me that you know this for certain to be true. Finn has escaped, he is no longer in prison."

He looked at her, his expression guileless as a babe's. "I swear."

"You are a true friend." She wheeled around and raced out of the store.

Brady watched her depart. He knew nothing about Finn MacGregor's whereabouts. He had scrawled the note when he'd seen her step into the store. What he told her wasn't entirely fabrication, for he did learn that Capitol Prison was in derelict condition and that security was lax. It was entirely possible that if her brother was half as bright as she, he had escaped to live another day.

Finn had escaped, after all, Finn, as great as his own legends! Now, walking to the village center, feeling the sun on her face, Anya felt her heart lift. Her brother had taken matters into his own hands and had revoked his own death sentence! Oh, to have him again by her side, to face the world together as they'd done as children.

On that balmy morning, Clayton was friendly, doors and windows flung open, women chatting with their neighbors as they hung quilts on lines for an airing. Anya lingered for awhile, watching over a fence as a young woman hoed her kitchen garden. She sang as she worked, and Anya thought that the woman must have faith to believe that anything would bear fruit in such a climate. A child toddled behind her, its dress trailing in the mud, poking at the ground with a stick. The woman felt Anya watching her and stood up, arching her back, hands on her hips. Anya saw that she was no more than her own age and that she carried another child.

The woman smiled at Anya, pushing her hair from her forehead. "With Ben's help, this will take twice as long."

"I was thinking that myself," Anya said, returning her smile. "He's been planting pebbles."

The woman laughed and scooped the lad up into her arms. "Benjamin! What will we eat this winter, stone soup?"

"Porr'ge!" he said. "Not stones."

Stone soup: an Irish feast. It was a bitter joke from the Famine years.

A year ago, Anya would have felt a flush of righteousness, but now she knew that the young woman meant no harm. Then the ferry whistle blew and Anya said goodbye and hurried down the street to the landing.

The pilot called out to her. "Saw you coming, miss! You'll be lucky to find a seat!"

Anya climbed over sacks of seeds and a cage of goslings to find a spot on the bench. She smiled her thanks to a farmer who moved to make room for her. It wasn't until she was seated that she noticed that he had a piglet inside his jacket. It snored softly, its eyes closed.

"It's me Pearl," the man confided. "She'll be the mother of dozens."

The passengers chatted companionably as they settled down for the journey back to Grindstone. As the ferry pulled away from the dock, the town receded, with its clamor of human activity. From a distance, Clayton reminded Anya of Donegal, with its docks filled with fishing boats and barges loaded with bales of wool. This time of year the hillsides would be covered with fuchsia, loud with lambs and meadowlarks returned at last to the barren land. The image was so clear that it could have been but a month ago that she had left Ireland, so lost to her now that it might be ten years.

As the ferry turned toward Grindstone, Anya noticed a boat approach then pass them by. A gust of wind filled the sail and the boat turned eastward, downriver, picking up speed. For a moment she imagined herself on the boat flying toward the sea.

She closed her eyes and thought of Jonathon, of how he had looked the morning he'd left. He had become a soldier again, he'd returned to battle, at least in his mind. Only a few days earlier she had been with him, her world turned upside down by a man she might never see again. She remembered what it had been like to lie in his arms, to lie beneath him as he looked into her eyes as they moved together as one. It had been worth it, she thought. She didn't regret it at all.

⋘⋙

As Douglas left the sailmaker's loft, he tucked the bundle under his arm, slinging his satchel over his shoulder. Making his way down along the shore, he spotted Annie coming up the path from Brady's Mercantile. She was smiling, twisting her hands with excitement like a young girl. He felt a surge of relief: Brady must have discovered good news about her brother. Distracted, she did not notice him, and he slipped into an alley and down the path to French Creek Bay.

His new skiff would not be ready for another week or two, but it would be worth the wait. The new boat was sturdy, rugged enough for the arduous journey downriver. He would have to be careful, find another island for his camp site, Wellesley, perhaps, still an easy row to Clayton. With so many veterans flooding the islands, he would be less conspicuous.

He rigged the sail on the old dinghy then pulled away from the dock. Then he hauled in the oars and let out the canvas, catching a westerly breeze. As the wind filled the sail, he scanned the town pier, noting which boats had landed, what cargo was being unloaded. Nothing unusual, as far as he could tell. He could see in the distance the stacks of a big steamer bearing down from Toronto, The Empress right on schedule. The island ferry was just ahead of him.

From beneath the sail he looked up at the deck. A woman stood alone at the railing, bonnet removed, dark hair catching the sunlight. She leaned into the railing, surveying the harbor. As she turned in his direction, he saw that it was Annie. He pulled in the sail, picking up speed, and turned the boat downriver so that he would not be seen.

CHAPTER 24

MORE THAN A WEEK PASSED before Anya stopped by the Burns farm, and when she saw the state of the place, she was stung with guilt. The kitchen was a horror, burnt pans on the stove, filthy dishes in the sink. It was obvious that Maddie was too young to keep house. Her eyes were shadowed, her mouth set, and Charlie was worse than ever, tormenting Riley, rocking mindlessly in his mother's chair.

"I hate it here," Maddie said. "My mother shouldn't have died." She stopped talking and looked more closely at Anya. Was she sick, too? Anya's skin was white as a ghost's, and she seemed to have trouble paying attention to anything she was saying. Maddie knew that Anya's husband had not returned from the war, but she didn't want to ask her about it, didn't want to make her friend sad.

They walked out to the pasture to look at the new calf, but Charlie was making such a pest of himself that she sent him off to pick beans for Anya to take back to her cabin. He ran to the kitchen garden, the puppy following at his heels.

"Where's Laddie?" Anya asked.

"Dead." Maddie shrugged and looked away. Then she asked Anya to come live with them. "School won't start for another month, and Michael is gone, he's living in Clayton, so he won't be a bother." She didn't mention the fight Michael had had with their father the night before he left, her father's look of bewilderment as his son crashed about the kitchen. Charlie had hid under the table in the unused parlor, and didn't come out until he heard Michael ride out of the yard and up the lane.

Maddie sighed. "Charlie is still horrid, but you could ignore him."

"Maddie, I can't," said Anya. "I'm going to look for work on the mainland at one of the new hotels. There's no way to make money here, I can't let the summer pass without saving anything."

"You could live with us and work in Clayton," Maddie said. "Then you wouldn't have to pay for food. You must be so lonely on your own." She paused. "Your cabin is scary. I bet there's bears."

Anya fished in her bag for the books she had brought from the schoolhouse. When she handed them to Maddie, the girl looked at her reproachfully. Maddie saw the gesture for what it was, a bribe, a sop to Anya's conscience. Anya had promised Cora that she would look after the children, and in her distress about Finn and Jonathon had all but forgotten them. The spark of childhood was gone in Maddie. It was the way of the world, Anya thought, but it was hard to see. The children had been left motherless too young.

A week later, Anya arose as the dawn broke and hiked down the path to the river. From the shore the islands were but shadows, only a strand of silver separating river from sky. It wasn't far to Clayton, and if she could paddle there, she would be able to save the ferry fare and the bit she paid Mr. Dodge for the ride from the landing. She would ask Brady for work, and if he had nothing, she would surely find something else. She couldn't cook, but she wasn't too proud for housekeeping. She pulled off her boots and stockings, setting them in the bow, then hiked up her skirts and hauled the dugout canoe into the river. Her hands on the gunwales to steady the boat, she climbed aboard, and with a few strokes, pulled away from the cove.

She'd had another sleepless night, lying awake listening to the loons. Her mind wandered dangerously at such times, worrying about Finn, dwelling on the night she had spent with Jonathon Douglas. It had begun to seem to her that the time with him had only been a dream, some fantasy she had contrived out of her loneliness. But as time passed, she began to understand the stark reality of her situation. She recognized the signs. She'd been old enough, when her mother was carrying Aisling, to know what pregnancy was.

To give herself courage, she sang as she paddled, a ballad she had heard on the journey across the ocean, sung by a lass as she nursed her wee babe.

> *Farewell to the groves of Shillelagh and Shamrock,*
> *Farewell to the wee boys of Ireland all around.*
> *May your hearts be as merry as ever I could wish for*
> *When it's far and away across the ocean I'm bound.*

Anya had never seen the groves of Shillelagh, she was not even certain where they were, but surely there were none lovelier than those in Donegal, where she had played among the standing stones with her brother, their mother reading, their father dozing in the sun. She set down her paddle. What would she do?

A woman's face appeared before her, summoned by her worries, the prostitute she had seen down by the wharves a few weeks earlier. Silently they had scrutinized each other, as if they had known each other in another life. Despite the painted cheeks and torn lace stockings, the woman might have been her own sister, they looked so alike.

"*Slainte*," the woman said.

"*Slainte*," Anya replied, then went on her way.

The steep slide to ruination. Was that how it happened?

In popular ballads, women in her situation had been fair warned:

> *Come all ye fair and tender ladies*
> *Take warning how you court your men*

They're like a star on a summer morning
First they appear and then they're gone.

All men are false, says my mother
They'll tell you sweet and loving lies
The next night, they'll court another
Leave you alone to pine and sigh.

Sometimes the foolish girls were murdered by their sweethearts, strangled or stabbed and dumped into the river for the inconvenience they caused by getting with child. Anya herself had sung such songs for her own entertainment. It had been a few weeks since she'd said good-bye to Douglas. It now seemed possible that she would never see him again.

So be it, she thought. She would not let her babe be called bastard, herself a whore. She would proudly raise it herself, she would say that her husband had finally returned, then headed west to find land for them. She would use Finn's enlistment money to support herself, as he would want her to do.

The enormity of it: she would have a child.

The mist had begun to clear, and as Anya looked about, she realized that it was here that she had heard the violin music drifting across the water. She remembered how comforted she had been by that unknown, kindred soul. Now she wondered if she had actually heard anything at all, if the music, as well, had been created by her loneliness.

The islands now looked forbidding, with their unfriendly shores, no curl of smoke above the trees. Then the sun began to burn off the morning mist, presaging a hot August day, and Anya turned her canoe back to Grindstone. She found that she was too tired to row to Clayton, a symptom, she knew, of early pregnancy. She would go another day.

From the rise, obscured by trees, he watched as the canoe headed away from his island. Annie was zig-zagging up the channel, paddling as if she had never managed a canoe before. What had possessed her to go out on the river on such a morning? The old dugout canoe was next to useless. If the wind came up she'd have a hard time getting back to Grindstone. And if the fog grew thicker she might head toward Clayton, blundering into a larger vessel making its way down the main channel..

He thought about the way she had looked that morning when he said goodbye, her dark hair falling about her shoulders, the hurt and anger in her eyes when she realized he had lied to her. He imagined her in that rough cabin, with her childhood journal, the chipped cups and two mended dresses. The letters from her brother, all she had left of him. Anya was alone in the world, without family or friends. By betraying her trust he had taken something more from her.

It wasn't enough to leave money for her, as if she were a whore. He must go to her now and tell her something of the truth before he left the islands. He owed her that much.

CHAPTER 25

SHE HAD BEEN SO INTENT on paddling that she did not hear him come upon her until he called her name. She turned in surprise. "Jonathon!" A smile lit her face. She paddled ashore then clambered out of the canoe and waited for him to land.

He made himself smile. "You hit the side of the canoe with each stroke! It's a crime for you to be out on the river."

She could not hide her joy. "I did not expect to see you again."

"I wish I could have come back sooner." He secured the skiff to a low-hanging branch then turned to her. "Anya, I have things to tell you, things you must know about me."

She saw that he was serious. "Are you married?" she asked, her voice cool.

It was not what he had expected. "No, I'm not married. I was betrothed before the war, but it was a long time ago. That doesn't matter now."

"Does she have any expectations of you?"

"No, none."

Anya nodded, then sitting on gunwale of the canoe brushed the sand from her feet and pulled on her stockings. She saw him look at her legs then away. Blushing, she covered them with her skirts and began to lace her boots. She could not have imagined that they would be awkward together. He looked out across the river, his arms folded, then after a moment, turned to her, shoving his hand through his hair.

She would not keep the truth from him, he had a right to know.

"Jonathon, I'm with child," she said.

He stared at her, stunned. "Annie, are you certain?"

"There's no doubt."

To his astonishment he felt a stab of joy. For a moment he couldn't speak. Then, "Is that why you came looking for me?"

"What are you talking about?"

He watched as the realization dawned on her.

"You've been living on that island all these months?" Her voice became steely. "I did not come searching for you, how would I know where to look? I never thought to see you again." To compose herself, she secured the canoe, stowing the paddles, tying the line around a tree trunk. Then she turned to him. "Why did you come to my cabin that evening? Why did you follow me this morning?"

He was again speechless. He had lied for so long, was so skilled at deception, he did not know what to say.

"I've come to tell you the truth," he said finally. "So you will know who I am."

Why was it impossible for them to be together? Why should he be denied what other men took for granted, to raise their child, to build a life together? It had already begun.

She looked at him, eyes wary, and then she nodded. He took her hand and together they hiked up the path to the highland, away from the cabin. Finding a place in the soft moss beneath the pines they lay together and for awhile they did not speak.

That night he told her that he had been a Confederate soldier and spy, and something of the episode in New York. Annie was troubled by the fact that he had betrayed his comrades, and so he told her more than he intended. He needed her to understand.

"An Englishman, Godfrey Hyams, approached us in Toronto. He'd come down from Nova Scotia with a trunk filled with clothes contaminated with smallpox. A doctor up there, a scoundrel named Blackburn, had arranged it. They were planning to send it to the White House, but if that failed, Hyams would donate the clothing to charity in New York and Philadelphia. Annie, when I was listening to Hyams, I kept thinking, Blackburn is a doctor, he knows how people die of smallpox, he knows how it will sweep through the slums."

"Did the others want to go along with it?"

"Thompson sent Hyams packing, but he still meant to go ahead with the bombings." He paused. "We were gathered around this table in a hotel in Toronto, talking about Greek fire, and I remembered this old man I'd seen on Hester Street. He was walking with a cane, holding the hand of his grandson, looking at the displays. It was cold, and the boy blew a cloud of vapor into the air, then laughed and did it again. I watched the grandfather bend and tuck the scarf around the boy's neck." He paused. "That's what I thought about when they were talking about firebombing the city." He looked at her. "Annie, I'm a surgeon. I couldn't go through with it."

She leaned against him, pulling his arms around her, placing his hands on her belly. "All that's over now," she said. "You must set it aside. Your children will be proud of what you have done."

The next morning they went to her cabin and gathered bedding and foodstuff. Then they rowed to Sorrow's Island, beyond the grass-covered drumlin on the northeast part of Grindstone where the Mississaugus camped in the summer. From the rise, they could see across to Howe Island and downriver to Eel Bay; they could identify any boat coming from Gananoque or Lake Ontario.

One morning he was building a fire on the small gravel beach to cook their morning catch, watching her skipping stones on the river. "Is it really possible you don't know how to swim?"

She laughed. "In Kilcar none of the fisherman could swim. The water was so cold that a body would drown in just a few minutes. That's why the wives knit fancy patterns in their jumpers, so their men could be recognized when their bodies were found."

"You will learn to swim. What if our baby falls into the water?" He took off his trousers, and slipping off her gown pulled her into the river. She laughed, gripping his neck so that he thought she might drown him as well. "Lie in my arms. Straighten your limbs. I won't let you go, I promise."

She couldn't relax. As soon as he lowered his arms she'd panic. "Close your eyes, try to relax. Trust me." No rush, they had all the time in the world.

After several tries she learned how to float, and with growing confidence began to paddle. The water was warm and smelled of grass, and she thought she'd never felt quite so free.

"So you are a merrow!" he said, laughing.

She swam away from him, then floated on her back looking at the sky. The clouds moved slowly, heading east, like the river. The world about her was constantly moving, only the granite islands anchoring her in the present. At night they lay together looking at the stars, the air sweet with pine and balsam. They talked about where they might settle, Nova Scotia, perhaps, or Maine on the coast of New England. She insisted that they live near the sea.

One night, as they drifted into sleep, she turned to him, her voice drowsy. "Is there anything else you haven't told me?"

"I'm a Jew."

She looked at him for a moment then settled back into his arms. "I don't know what it means to be a Jew. There were none in my village, the priest preached against them."

"Would your parents have minded you marrying me?"

"I don't know. They would have worried. My mother was a Catholic and my father Protestant, and their own parents were furious when they eloped. But it doesn't matter, my mother and father are dead." She paused. "What about your family? Will they mind?"

Before the war it would have been impossible. He pulled her to him. "You are my family now."

CHAPTER 26

FROM THE DOCKS OF KINGSTON, Kennedy and his men watched another storm roll down Lake Ontario, black clouds roiling over Wolfe Island. The lake was churned to a froth, waves slamming the quays. The squall was heading downriver, and they could see lightning strikes in the distance, like artillery. If only it were a bombardment, Kennedy thought, pounding the cities and villages of the North.

There was nothing left of the South. Great fields of wheat and cotton, wasted, homes looted then torched. What livestock had not been stolen was slaughtered for no other reason than to punish the families of those who had fought for the Confederacy. Just as they had hanged Mary Surratt for the patriotism of her husband. He had read last week the newspaper accounts of the executions, the lurid headlines: LINCOLN ASSASSINS HANGED. Editors expressed "universal repugnance to hanging a woman," yet many begged for passes to witness the event. The grotesque photograph was published for all the world to see. The Northerners were a despicable people. Their brutality would not be forgotten.

A crowd had gathered at a street corner around a man who had made a platform of out of a packing crate. "Ontario's Independence from England!" he shouted. "The time has come! Throw off the yoke of tyranny. Freedom is within our reach!" Good luck to them, Kennedy thought bitterly. He remembered such men rallying support for the Southern Cause. It seemed a lifetime ago. All that was left were the ashes.

Searching for Douglas, he and his men had scoured the taverns, the shipyards, the boarding houses on Queen Street, down by the river and up the hill where the newcomers lived. In the small enclave of Jews, no one could identify the man in the drawing. It was not surprising. Kingston was not the sort of place he'd hole up in for any length of time. They would move on to Gananoque, a smaller village on the St. Lawrence. It was possible that he had staked a claim along the river, had found a cabin where he could live unnoticed, hunting and fishing, where he could escape by boat. They would search, one by one, the thousand islands along the border between the United States and Canada.

Kennedy lay awake every night reliving his brother's murder, Robbie's jaunty, simple farewell, his fearless drop into the void. Kennedy went over the nights before the betrayal, the way Douglas had set them up, using his skill to betray them all.

When had Douglas changed his mind? The man had fought for the Confederacy, had risked his life pulling injured men from the battlefield. It wasn't money that had swayed him, he wasn't the sort. It must have been some confused sense of principle, some profound change or weakening of the heart. It angered Kennedy that he, all of them, had been so easily fooled. In his more rational moments, Kennedy recognized that Thompson was not an able leader, that their plan to firebomb New York had been desperate and ill-considered, but ultimately he blamed Douglas not only for the death of his brother but for the loss of the Confederacy, the destruction of the South.

As clever as Douglas was, he would make a mistake. He had been on the run for a long time. He would grow weary of the deceit and let down his guard. He would run out of money and need to find work. Then too, an isolated young man far from home would eventually seek female companionship, and through this connection, they might well find him.

CHAPTER 27

THE DAY OF THEIR DEPARTURE was almost upon them. Anya and Jonathon packed up their gear and hiked together down to the shore of Sorrow's Island. She sat in the bow of the boat, watching him as he rowed back to Grindstone. His face was as tanned as a fisherman's and his curly hair glinted in the sun. He noticed her looking at him and laughed aloud. She had cut his hair so that he looked more presentable, but she hadn't been able to convince him to shave his beard. She wanted to see the line of his jaw, something of what he had looked like as a lad. She knew the way his skin felt, the scar on his back. It seemed to her that she had known him all her life.

He pulled into the cove then climbed out of the boat, helping her alight. "I'll come back for you tomorrow," he said. "The skiff should be ready. While I'm in Clayton I'll purchase what we need for the trip. "

"I need to go there myself, to leave a message for my brother. Why can't we just go together?"

"We must not be seen together." He paused. "Annie, it would be better if you sent Brady a message when we are well on our way."

"I can't run off without leaving word for my brother! Seamus won't betray us."

He did not like the plan, but it was obvious that he could not argue her out of it. "Annie, you must be very discreet, you must give Brady no clues." He took her hands. "You must believe that the men who are pursuing me are dangerous, and that they are now a danger to you."

The urgency in his voice unsettled her. "I will be careful, Jonathon."

"Here, let me carry this gear up to your cabin."

"I can manage. You should go."

Then he pulled her to him and held her tight. She wrapped her arms around him and closed her eyes, inhaling the smell of his hair, his skin, feeling his strength.

She watched as he headed back to his island until all she could see was the white speck of his shirt. The dawn was glorious, the sun glinting on the water, turning the river to gold. Tomorrow they would be on their way. She gathered their things and hiked the rise to her cabin.

The day promised to be another hot one; already her gown was dragging on her legs. She noted another tear in the fabric; she would need to wash and mend her dress before going into town. In the sun it would dry in less than an hour. She wished that she had something more presentable to wear on their journey, but there was no point, they would be camping until they reached their destination. Jonathon promised that when they got to Maine he would buy her something pretty. "Something loose!" she said. "This one is already snug in the waist." In a few months she would be able to feel the baby's movements. She hoped for a girl. She still remembered Aisling as a baby, with her downy hair and sweet smile.

As Anya approached the yard, she heard a muffled crack, a stick breaking, then another. Someone was edging his way along the woods. Anya looked back toward the water. But Jonathon was well on his way, and in any case, she could not reveal his presence.

A man stepped from the shadows. He was stocky, dressed in a filthy coat. As he touched his cap she could see that he'd lost two fingers from his right hand. "'Morning, miss." He smiled to reassure her. He was missing several teeth. He gestured to her gear. "Looks like you been out on a camping trip. All by yourself?" He nodded to her cabin. "Made use of the overhang on account of the rain. Hope you don't mind." He chuckled benignly.

Anya looked at her cabin then at the man, not knowing what to say. His explanation made no sense. It had rained hours ago. He wasn't carrying any fishing gear and they hadn't seen his boat when they'd approached the island. She tried to remain calm, to seem unafraid.

He shifted his rucksack. "Thought it was a trapper camp."

"Did you go inside?"

"No, miss. Just used the overhang is all."

She knew he was lying. "The schoolmaster lives over there, in the schoolhouse. And the neighbors are just beyond."

He grinned, showing her the obviousness of her fabrication. "Well, that's good. Myself, I wouldn't want to live alone in such a place. You see any strangers, miss?" He chuckled again. "Aside from myself?"

"You don't have any business here." To her own ears, her voice sounded frightened. "Leave at once," she said coldly.

Instead of leaving, he looked about the yard. "Well, I do have business, miss. I'm an agent, I guess you would say. A federal agent." He folded his arms. "Used to hunt escaped Rebs down from the prison on Wellesley. Now I'm hunting traitors." He spat into the bushes. "Deserters. You know any hereabouts?"

"No. I don't know anyone. Leave now."

"All right, then." He put on his hat. "I'll be back this way. If you find out anything, they'll be something in it for you." He touched his cap. "Name's Warner Blunt, by the way. And yours?" When she didn't respond, he laughed and went on his way, heading toward the road.

Anya willed herself to stand firm as he left the clearing, listening for the man's footsteps as he crossed the bridge. After a few minutes, she ran into the cabin and bolted the door. He must have come ashore up island, walking randomly from house to house looking for prey. Was he truly a bounty hunter or was he one of the men pursuing Jonathon? If that were the case, Blunt had missed him by only a few minutes. Should she row to Maple and warn him? Blunt might be watching her cabin even now, might be down by the shore. She would proceed with their original plan.

Anya slung the quilt over the line then hurriedly packed her things. She collected her books, tucking Erik's drawing inside one of the covers, then slipped them into the carpet bag with her shell box and winter gown. She set about tidying the cabin. As she looked around, she realized that she would be leaving Grindstone with little more than when she'd arrived. Still, the carpet bag contained all of her worldly goods, and so she went outside and stashed it under the cabin where it was less likely to be noticed.

As for the money, it was too risky carrying so many bank notes on their journey, so she decided that she would leave the tin with Angus Burns; she would stop at the farm on her way to the ferry and leave Finn's clothing as well. She would explain that she would be away for awhile visiting relatives. If Finn appeared in her absence, Angus should give him the money and the clothing. It would pain her to say goodbye to the Burns family, but it was something she would not write in a letter.

She dug up the tin and put it in her purse then folded Finn's clothing into a pillow slip. Tucking it under her arm, she hiked up the path to the lane. The sun was already high in the sky, and the leaves were beginning to wilt in the heat. Anya turned and looked back at her clearing. Though it had been her home for almost a year, the cabin looked forlorn, unattended. The little kitchen garden she had started was pathetic—with all of the trees there was not enough sun to grow a radish.

The island road was so dry that as she walked along her boots kicked up clouds of dust. The sky was empty of birds. A few storms had blown through in the past few weeks, but they moved too quickly to serve much purpose. Without more rain the crops would be stunted to the point of ruin.

From a distance the Burns's farmhouse looked dark and unwelcoming. The doors and windows were shut to keep out the heat, and the livestock huddled in the shade of the big elm. Then the door flew open and Charlie raced up the lane to meet her, the pup at his heels.

Charlie tugged her down the path, the pup barking, racing around in circles. Maddie stepped onto the porch and threw the burnt morning biscuits out into the yard. She looked at Anya, noting the bundle she carried. "Have you come to stay with us? Is that why you've brought your things?"

Anya shook her head, trying to ignore the hope in the girl's voice. "Is your father here?"

"He's over to the mill getting some shakes for the roof. It leaks. If Michael would come back and help, we wouldn't be in such a fix. I burned the porridge, too. That's why the house smells so bad."

"Maddie. I came to say goodbye. I'll be gone for awhile, but I will write to you."

Maddie stared at her. "What about school? Will you be back to open it?"

Anya wanted to lie, to spare Maddie the disappointment. "No, Maddie. I will write to Mr. Hanson to let him know. He will find you another teacher, a proper one." She touched the girl's shoulder, but Maddie pulled away from her.

"All right, then," said Maddie. "Goodbye."

Anya turned to the boy. "Charlie, do you think you can find us some eggs for breakfast?"

He nodded and raced to the henhouse, the gate slamming behind him.

"Maddie, are you my friend?"

The girl looked at her in surprise. "Yes."

"I need your help. Will you help me? It's important."

Maddie nodded. Anya did not tell her about Jonathon, only that she would not be returning to the island, at least in the next year or two. "Another thing you must know. Finn is not my husband, he's my brother."

Maddie's eyes widened at the enormity of her schoolmistress having told such a lie.

"It's the way of the world, Maddie. The islanders would not have hired an unmarried girl."

Maddie knew this to be true. "I won't tell a living soul."

Anya told Maddie about Finn's conscription money, and together they decided on a place to hide the tin so that when Finn appeared, he would be able to make use of it. "And these are his clothes. You must give them to him. Our mother wove the shirt herself."

"Anya, will I ever see you again?" Maddie's eyes filled with tears.

Anya pulled her close. She did not want Maddie to wait for her, as she waited for Finn. "I hope so, Maddie, but it may be a long time. But I will write to you."

Charlie whooped back into the house carrying three eggs, one broken. "This is all there were. Why are you crying?"

"Goodbye, Charlie. Promise me you'll learn to read." She smiled at him. She knew that if she tried to hug him he would wriggle away in horror. She turned again to Maddie. "Your mother was my friend. She was good to me, and I will never forget her kindness. She would be very proud of you." She smoothed the girl's hair. "Don't give up your lessons, even if you don't like your new teacher."

Charlie interrupted. "Don't you want the eggs?"

"I'm sorry, Charlie. I need to catch the ferry. Say goodbye to your da and tell him thank you for everything. I wish I could have told him myself." She turned and ran up the lane to the island road. With any luck she would catch Emmet Dodge on his trip to the landing.

In Clayton, the weather was even sultrier than on the island. Men wore shirtsleeves and women had set aside their wide-brimmed bonnets for more perfunctory head coverings. Village dogs slept away the day under the porches of Hubbard House and the other hotels, and horses flicked flies with their tails in the shade of the elms that lined James Street. Even the maples drooped in the heat, and the bay simmered under a colorless sky.

When Anya arrived at Brady's Mercantile, the shop was empty, Brady leaning against the counter reading the newspaper. He looked up in surprise as she approached the counter. "Mrs. MacGregor! You're like a sea breeze on this hot day."

The lass looked different, girlish. Her skin was darker, she'd been too much in the sun, but it was becoming. Her figure was fuller, her features softened, and despite her impatience, she seemed more at ease, as if she'd finally ceased doing battle with the world. So he found himself snorting in disbelief at her first words.

"Mr. Brady, I need a pistol."

"You've been living out there without a weapon?"

"I've a shotgun but it's only a boy's. I need a real gun, something I can carry in my pocket." She paused. "A man came to my cabin this morning. He said he was a bounty hunter. Warner Blunt was his name, or at least that's what he said. He was horrible."

Brady's voice was terse. "Did he molest you in any way?"

"No," she said impatiently. "He wanted to know if I had seen any deserters."

He felt the rage course through him. "Thinking to waylay some poor sod who's made his way alive back from hell." He leaned onto the counter. "I wish my Conor had taken off when he'd had the chance. And I'd kill with my own hands the likes of Blunt who'd drag him to prison for saving his own life. By God I will kill him if he steps foot in my store." Brady's face was red with anger. "A pistol won't help you! Men like Blunt are all over the islands now, like a disease. Mrs. MacGregor, you know you can't live out there anymore, not on your own. Live in town, work for me. I know of a respectable boarding house."

She wished she could tell him the truth, that she'd be on her way the very next morning. She shook her head.

"All right, I can sell you a gun, but you need a dog as well. I know someone who's got a mastiff bitch with a new litter. I could get you a pup for nothing."

"No dog."

He regarded her for a moment then went into the back room, returning with a leather case. He laid it on the counter for her to look at, then pulled out a small revolver. "This is a Derringer, small enough for you to manage, big enough to take the nose off the Blunts of the world." He held it out to her. "You see, he couldn't wrestle it from you, as he might a bigger gun. It fits right in the palm of a lady's hand." He pulled out a drawer and counted out a number of bullets. "These are .22's. That's what you'll need. The pistol takes only two bullets, so you'd have to stand close to hit the target." He looked at her. "Only two chances. Could you do it, shoot a man in the chest?"

She thought of Blunt's leering face. "Aye."

He loaded the bullets into the chambers.

"That's it?"

"That's all it takes. Cock the hammer, pull the trigger. Come along with me." He locked the front door and pulled the shade. Anya followed him through the back room and out into the empty lot behind the store. Brady propped a hay bale against a tree. He stepped back a dozen yards, then emptied the pistol and handed it to her, along with the bullets. "Now load it."

She fumbled the first time, dropping the bullets on the ground. Impatiently she picked them up, then loaded them properly.

"Do as I told you."

When she pulled the trigger, the gun seemed to explode in her hand.

"Again."

This time, she flinched before she pulled the trigger, jerking upward, hitting the top of the trees.

"Again," he said, reloading. "Two in a row."

Anya hit nowhere near the target. Brady laughed. "You'll need more practice, Mrs. MacGregor. But you'll get it soon enough."

When they returned to the store, Anya watched as he filled the small leather pouch with bullets. "How much is it?"

"Not for sale." He polished the pistol with a clean rag, then replaced it in its leather case. "It was my wife's, I wouldn't sell it for a hundred gold coins. If I had a daughter of my own, I'd give it to her." He slid it across to her. "You can pay for the bullets, though. Twenty cents."

"Mr. Brady—"

"Promise me you'll practice. So if you panic, you don't shoot your own foot. I'll hear from my wife in Kingdom Come if you do something foolish with her pistol." He laughed. "Look, if it makes you feel beholden, help me sort my bills at the end of the month." He nodded to the impaled notes on the counter.

She looked at him. "Thank you, Mr. Brady." Then she went about the store gathering small provisions that they would need, cheese, bread, coffee, lard. Finally she pulled the envelope from her satchel. "Mr. Brady, if my brother comes looking for me, please give him this letter."

"You think I wouldn't send him straight to you?"

She smiled. "It's to welcome him. So he knows I haven't forgotten him."

He watched as she hurried from the store. Something was afoot, that was for certain. The lass could hardly contain her excitement. He opened the letter and began to read. She'd written it in *Gaelige*, but he hadn't forgotten his own language.

On her way past the shipbuilders' docks, Anya looked for Jonathon, hoping that the skiff was finished and that he was already well on his way back to Maple. If only there were a way to let him know about Blunt.

When she got to the ferry landing she had to stand in line. Several passengers crowded the ramp, jostling as they stepped onto the boat. Anya spotted Erik Karlson ahead of her, leading a calf, and found a seat beside him. Meg Robinson's mother sat down next to her. Then the island blacksmith wheeled an anvil on board, causing the ferry to rock then right itself.

The pilot frowned. Normally he would not allow such weight with so many passengers, but the river was dead calm. "All right, then." As the old man waited for one barge, then the next to pull away from the dock, he kept glancing at the opal-colored sky. "Don't like it," he muttered, mopping his brow. "Don't like it one bit."

"It's awful close," said Mrs. Robinson, fanning herself. Sweat poured down her neck. "I can hardly catch my breath."

Anya realized that she, too, was breathless, as if something were pressing on her chest. She lifted her hair from her neck then turned to Erik. "I've missed you since school has ended. What a pretty calf."

He stroked it between the ears. "Papa sent me to get it," he said proudly. "I paid the man and everything."

"Well, you're a good help to your da."

The calf bawled as the ferry pulled away from the village, Erik shushing it as if it were a child. The air was so hazy that Anya could see only faded color and movement on the quay. The harbor was crowded with vessels of all sorts, sailing ships and steamers and barges loaded to the decks.

She closed her eyes, lulled by the movement of the ferry. Then she noticed that the air had begun to freshen. She opened her eyes to see gulls soaring downriver. A family of diving ducks hurried by, the mother anxiously scolding her ducklings. Anya stood, suddenly chilled, and gasped when she looked upriver.

A line of clouds had gathered over the head of Grindstone and was sweeping toward them, bringing a wall of rain. The storm moved in with a ferocity that stunned them, waves dashing against themselves, rolling in from the west, growing before their eyes. A bolt of lightning struck Calumet and a tree burst into flames. Someone screamed. Erik took Anya's hand, and she gripped it tightly.

Then a wave slapped them broadside, and the anvil slid across the deck, crashing into the railing. The wood splintered and cracked, and then the ferry tipped on its side, spilling the anvil into the river. Another wave washed over the bow and the boat began to go down.

CHAPTER 28

WHEN HE LOOKED TO THE WEST, he saw it all of a piece, like some metaphorical painting: the linear storm cloud, demonic, building with unbelievable speed in a yellow sky. The roiling bay, a welter of blue-green foam. He jerked the rudder, heading toward land, Bluff Island looming before him. The boom swung around, and the canvas caught hold. He shifted his weight, leaning back, offsetting the pressure as much as he could. The skies opened up, and the rain came down. Lightning crackled overhead, followed by a boom.

Approaching the shore, he dropped the sail and rowed as fast as he could. A wave lifted the skiff, then another, slamming it, threatening to capsize it. He jumped waist deep into the water and gripping the gunwale, wrestled the skiff ashore. The waves drove hard against him, the green rain horizontal. Thunder boomed around him like the detonation of a cannon.

He found cover under an overhang, the trees groaning and snapping overhead. Amid cracks of lightning, thunder shook the air around him. A bolt hit a tall pine, shaving the trunk from crown to roots like a giant plane. Then he heard a tremendous roar. It seemed as if the Angel of Judgment was passing overhead in a fury of retribution.

Then the wind ceased and all was silent. After awhile, birds began to twitter, a loon called anxiously for its chicks. From the shore, he could see the mass of black clouds roiling downriver. Then he heard the cries for help. Looking toward Clayton he saw that the ferry had capsized. Although the boat was not far from the mainland, the current was swift.

Clearly it was going down.

He pulled the mast and rigging from the skiff and stashed them in the woods. Then he hauled his boat into the water and headed toward the ferry. As he pulled on the oars, he realized that Annie might be aboard.

As he approached the wreck, he could see that the boat was partly submerged, drifting down the channel. Passengers crowded the upraised bow calling for help. By now rescue boats from Clayton had reached the ferry, and in anticipation, a few men had climbed over the side, dropping into the water, swimming to meet them.

Douglas pulled near the ferry, looking for Annie. The waves were washing over the deck, and he could see the old pilot trying to calm the remaining passengers. When he spotted Douglas he called out to him. "How many can you carry?"

"I can take three. Is the schoolmistress aboard?"

The old man shook his head. "Don't think so." He reached down and grabbed the gunwales, stabilizing the skiff against the ferry. "Here, you," he said to the woman next to him. She climbed over the railing and steadying herself, boarded the skiff. Once in her seat, she called out for her children, and the ferryman lowered two little girls onto her lap.

When she had settled them on the bottom of the skiff, Douglas shoved the skiff away from the ferry and rowed around to the other side. He scanned the water and the deck looking for her, but the river was now crowded with boats, and so he pulled away from the mayhem and rowed back to Clayton with his passengers. The ferry had drifted downriver; the closest point of land was just above Goose Bay. He'd be less conspicuous there, and it would be only a short hike into the village.

The little girls gripped the gunwales, looking about, wide eyed, in silence. Their mother, who looked little older than Annie, smiled shyly at Douglas, then looked back at the wreck.

Douglas rowed the skiff into a small inlet, then climbed out and pulled it into the reeds. Then he helped the woman and children alight.

"Thank you," she said. "You are a blessing from the Lord."

The landing was crowded, people milling about, shouting and pointing at the rescue boats. Douglas pushed his way through for a better view of the docks. Ferry passengers were making their way up the ramps, moving slowly, looking back at the almost submerged ferry. There he spotted Annie. She was with a boy, her arm about his shoulder, obviously trying to comfort him.

"Annie," he shouted. When he reached her, he pulled her close. "I looked for you at the wreck."

"I know, I saw you. I called but you couldn't hear me."

"You're sound?"

She nodded. "Aye, but Erik is hurt. Is there something you can do?"

Douglas saw, then, that the boy had a bad gash on his arm and was trying hard not to cry.

"I lost my calf," he said.

Douglas examined the wound, then tore a strip of cloth from his own shirt and quickly bandaged the boy's arm. "When you get home, you must have your mother clean the cut and find another bandage. Can you manage that?"

"The storm came, and my calf was shaking, she was really scared." His eyes filled with tears. "I lost hold of her when the wave hit."

"Annie, we need to leave right now. My skiff's down river just below the village."

"Let me see if I can find someone to keep track of Erik. I can't leave him on his own." She began surveying the crowd.

It was then that she spotted him. Warner Blunt was talking to one of the dockworkers, laughing and shaking his head. She gripped Jonathon's arm and pulled him into the crowd. "There's a man over there," she whispered. "He was at my cabin this morning, just after you left. He said he was looking for deserters."

Jonathon bent his head low. "Did he see you just now?"

"I don't know. I can't be certain."

"Tell me what he looks like."

"A red beard, heavy-set. He's missing two fingers. He called himself Warner Blunt."

Douglas knew the man. He'd seen him once or twice with Robbie Kennedy in New York the previous winter. He pulled some money from his pocket. "Find a place to stay tonight."

"I want to go with you."

"No, it's not safe. Are you certain you're sound?"

She nodded.

"We'll meet here tomorrow. There must be a Catholic Church where you can wait."

"Aye, St. Mary's, near the public square. What time?"

"Six o'clock tomorrow evening. We'll leave just after sunset."

She gripped his hands. "Tomorrow at six. I will be waiting for you in the back of the church."

CHAPTER 29

IT WAS A LUCKY BREAK, the first they'd had in two months of searching. Kennedy had left a man in Kingston and sent Blunt across the lake to Cape Vincent, where he would board the train to Clayton. That left Kennedy with two men to scour the rugged areas that fronted the river, going from cabin to shop to farmhouse, showing the traitor's likeness.

When they reached Gananoque, a village on the Canadian side of the river, they found a shopkeeper who recognized Douglas. He spoke at length about the traveler who had come through the previous November. He remembered him because he had spent so much money. "Looked to me like he was plannin' to set up housekeeping somewhere. Bought enough to last for weeks. Flour, coffee, kerosene."

"Was he alone?"

"He was."

"On horseback?"

The old man chuckled. "That was the funny thing. He didn't have nothin', no horse, no wagon. Dressed pretty fine, I'd say, for a man without a mount. I watched him out the window. He packed the goods in a duffle and hefted it onto his back and set off down the road. Had a fiddle with him!"

"Seen anything of him since then?"

"Nope. I was hoping to—the man was a good customer. Why are you lookin' for him?"

Kennedy smiled. "He was in our regiment. He's gone missing and his wife is looking for him."

"Maybe he don't want to be found. Wouldn't be the first."

Then Kennedy paid the man for his troubles. "If you see him again, don't mention we're looking for him. He's easily spooked." He tapped his head.

The storekeeper tucked the bills into his money box. Of course he could keep his mouth shut. Easiest thing in the world. Just don't open it.

When they got to the tavern where they had taken rooms, Kennedy spread the map of the river on the table.

Ramsey shook his head. "Look at all these islands. The perfect place to hide."

Tom Kennedy scrutinized the map. Opposite Gananoque, on the American side was the village of Clayton. Between the American and Canadian shores were hundreds of lesser islands, and amid them, two larger ones, Grindstone and Wellesley. Downriver, hundreds more, thinning out as the St. Lawrence made its way to Montreal. He drew a ten mile radius around the area. "This is where we'll find him. He'll be here, close to the villages and the trains."

"You really think he's still in the country?"

Kennedy nodded. "Better than even chance. This is the perfect place to hide."

"Why don't he just go back to Richmond?"

"He knows he's a dead man as soon as he crosses into Virginia." Kennedy folded up the map. "Blunt should be in Clayton by now. Let's head across the river from here, and meet up with him, see what he's found."

CHAPTER 30

AFTER HE LEFT ANNIE ON THE LANDING, Douglas pulled his hat low and edged away from the crowd. He headed inland down Merrick Street, then made his way cross-lots to Franklin. Sensing that he was being followed, he slowed his pace and glanced back. Blunt was a few blocks behind him, pausing on the street corner pretending to read a billboard. Douglas pulled a knife from his boot top and continued on his way. When he rounded a corner, he stepped into the doorway of an iron monger's shop. He could hear Blunt making his way down the gravely path.

When Blunt rounded the corner, Douglas was waiting for him. Douglas struck swiftly, sending the blade into the base of the man's throat. Blunt looked at him in surprise; it was over in a few seconds. Douglas dragged the body behind the shop to the river bank and shoved it over the edge. It rolled down the embankment and lodged in the cattails. Then he made his way down the path to where his skiff was hidden and shoving it into the river, climbed aboard.

He had no way of knowing how many men were with Blunt, but it was clear Kennedy was close by. He pulled on the oars, heading downriver past Round Island. When he was sure he was not being followed, he turned, rowing across the channel toward Maple. The more distance he could put between himself and Annie, the safer she would be.

Anya watched Jonathon vanish into the crowd. Then she looked about the landing for Blunt. The man had already disappeared. Willing herself to be calm, Anya turned to the boy. "Erik, you need to head back to Grindstone. Let's go down to the dock and see if there's another boat."

"I'm all right now. I can go on my own."

"I know, but I'd like to walk with you." She could hear the urgency in her own voice.

"Who was that man you were talking to?"

"A friend."

"He was nice."

With the excitement over, the crowd began to clear. Once again boats filled the river, a large steamship making its way down the channel. Anya went with Erik down to one of the small piers, looking about for Blunt. She didn't know what she would do if she saw him, but at least she would know that Jonathon was safe.

A leather-skinned old farmer joined them on the landing. "They're sending another ferry."

"The lad needs a ride back."

"Bad business about the pilot."

"What?"

"Collapsed on the pier. Must have been his heart give way." He shook his head. "Old fellow ran the ferry for as long as anyone could remember."

Anya recognized him then, the grandfather of one of her students. She looked at Erik, but the boy seemed not to have heard. He was fiddling with the bandage on his arm, a distraught look on his face. "I hope Papa doesn't punish me."

"It wasn't your fault, was it then? Nobody's fault."

He nodded uncertainly. "Mrs. MacGregor, I want to come back to school. But Mother said that I am needed at home, now that I am grown."

The boy was no more grown than a colt and with little more learning. Anya felt a stab of anger. But what could she say? She had no right to say anything. She was leaving, she wouldn't be there to teach any of them.

"I could help you after school, with the stove and all. I would be a good help to you, Mrs. MacGregor. I'm a grown boy."

"Aye, I know you are." She paused. "I hope you'll continue to draw. I treasure the picture you gave me." Then she smiled. "I need to go. You'll be all right, then? Do you have money to get back?"

He fished in his pocket and pulled out a quarter.

She touched his shoulder. "Goodbye, Erik." Then she hurried up the ramp to the landing.

Anya looked about the village center for a room for the night, but the town was crowded and most of the hotels were full. She finally found a decent enough inn down near the shipyards. Even in that rougher neighborhood, the clerk looked her up and down, frowning when he heard her accent, but he took her money readily enough.

The clerk did not bother to escort her to her room, and it was no surprise that he had given her a tiny one under the eaves. It was probably used by the maids when it wasn't needed by guests. It was sweltering, airless, and she opened the small window knowing it was useless. Then she went down the back stairs and out onto the street. She was worried about running into Blunt, but she was hungry, she hadn't eaten since that morning. She didn't have the courage to enter a tavern on her own and hoped Brady's would still be open for business.

Brady's Mercantile was indeed open, packed with customers. Brady had hired a couple of musician, and the fiddler and drummer sat on cracker barrels out on the porch, playing to attract business. A bottle of whisky made the rounds, and the talk was lively. As Anya moved to the counter, she began listening to the gossip swirling around her. Voices were loud with excitement, interrupting one another. There was something about a murder, about a body that had been found that very evening by fishermen in the cattail reeds in Goose Bay. The man's throat had been cut.

Someone said he was a foreigner who had been shoved from a steamer. "Couldn't be," another pointed out. "If he fell off one of the steamers, he'd bloat up and float downriver."

"Could've been blown ashore by the storm."

"You saw that piece in *the Times*. Lincoln's assassins are hiding out right here in the islands. Could be one of them bastards."

Brady leaned over the counter. "The lot of you are full of shite. Was likely a brawl over cards. Or a whore. A soldier gets through the worst of it in battle then throws away his life over a bad hand of poker." Then he noticed Anya. "Were you on that ferry that went down?"

She nodded distractedly. "Do you know who the murdered man was?" she asked, trying to keep the fear from her voice.

Brady looked at her. "He was a fat sack of shite and he was missing two fingers."

Her eyes widened. "The man at my cabin!"

"So you won't be worryin' about him, will you then? His deviltry caught up with him."

She lowered her voice. "Mr. Brady, did you kill him?"

He laughed. "If I had, I surely wouldn't tell you! But I would have welcomed the chance, the bastard." He paused. "Still have that pistol?"

She'd forgotten all about it, and instinctively patted for it. "It's in my pocket."

"There's a lass." He already knew from the letter she'd left for Finn MacGregor that she was leaving the islands. She'd tried to camouflage the details, but she wasn't very good at lying. He wondered if she was running off with a man—that would account for the bloom in her cheeks the other morning. Now she looked woebegone, all the light gone out of her.

"I'd like some cheese and bread. And if you have an apple."

"You're not going back to the island tonight?"

"I'm staying in Clayton in one of the inns."

"Just wait here a minute." He went over to one of the shelves and pulled out a shawl. "It's just come in. Pretty color, pinkish, I'd say. You can't be goin' about in the evenin' without cover, Mrs. MacGregor. It's not decent."

"I don't have enough money."

He smiled. "It's meant as a gift."

"Thank you, Mr. Brady. And you have my letter."

"I do. It's safe with me. *Go mbeannaí Dia duit,*" he said. May God bless you.

She touched his hand. "*Go mbeannaí Dia is Muire duit.* You're a good man, Mr. Brady."

He was more than certain this was not the case, but it was nice to hear it, all the same. He would miss this one.

The night air was damp as she made her way back to the inn, and she was glad for the shawl to cover her hair. As it was, men were staring at her as she passed by. The clerk was dozing in his chair when she entered the hotel and she slipped up the stairs unnoticed.

Her room was still stuffy, even with the window open, and Anya removed her gown and hung it on a hook, smoothing it as best she could. The water in the pitcher was stale, but she was able to wash with the sliver of soap left in the dish. She brushed the tangles from her hair, then lay down on the bed. The sheets smelled sour, and so she tugged the chair by the window and sat down, suddenly aware that she was exhausted.

The waterfront was bright with torch light, and laugher and music filled the night. Every now and then shouts erupted from the taverns. Had Jonathon killed Blunt? Was he safe? She had no way of knowing. After awhile, she pulled her shawl around herself and lay down on the bed. For the baby's sake, she must rest. She lay on her side, cradling her belly, willing herself to sleep.

CHAPTER 31

AT THE FREIGHT YARD IN CLAYTON, Michael Burns checked items from an inventory list of goods being unloaded from the train. The foreman had fought with the 94th and had given him the job. Michael was grateful for the work; the money wasn't bad, and he could sleep for next to nothing in a bunkhouse near the yard, eating in the mess with the other veterans.

It troubled him that he had left the farm in such a poor state, but he had not been of much use to his father and felt bad that he had lost his temper that night. He would stop by with his wages as soon as he was paid. The incident at Anya MacGregor's cabin had clarified for him that there was no other reason for him to remain on the island.

The day his regiment had returned, he'd been caught up with his comrades and lost track of her in the crowd. He had looked for her along the platform and then the docks and finally headed back to Grindstone on his own. The next morning he had gone to her cabin to find out what had happened. He wasn't a fool—when she emerged, face flushed, hair hanging down, her bodice undone, he knew at once that someone had spent the night with her. After an awkward conversation, he left, but then doubled back, hiding in the cover of the trees. Sure enough, a man stepped out of the cabin, wary, guilty as sin. It was the man he had seen with her that winter in Clayton.

Who was he? And what business did he have with Anya MacGregor? Well, that was no mystery. How long had her husband been gone for a soldier? Long enough, apparently, for her to give up waiting for him.

Caught up in his thoughts, he did not take particular notice of the three men stepping off the train. There was nothing remarkable about them, in any case, nothing to draw his attention. Their clothes were nondescript, and they did not communicate with one another in an obvious way.

Kennedy watched the freight worker move awkwardly back and forth among the cars, favoring one leg. Kennedy waited for a lull in his activity before approaching him.

"Don't I know you, son?" he said, with an affable grin.

Michael looked at him blankly. "Don't think so. Were you in the 94th?"

"We didn't fight together. You never forget the faces of the men you fought with." He paused, his expression sober. "It was in the hospital."

"In Washington?"

The man nodded. "You were pretty much out of your mind, I'd say, with the surgery and all. Not surprised you don't remember."

"What were you doing there?"

"Nothin' much. I was lucky." He instinctively rubbed his shoulder. Then the man wiped his brow with his hat and looked around. "I'm looking for someone," he said finally. "You being from hereabouts might be able to help a fellow veteran." He pulled out a folded leather case and removed a sketch. "You seen this man?"

Michael looked at the drawing then up at the stranger. "What's your business with him?"

"I'm not a bounty hunter, if that's what you're thinking. Them's the foulest creatures that ever crawled the earth."

Michael reached for the drawing and looked at it more closely. After a moment, he said, "You didn't say what your business was."

"He's my sister's husband, gone almost a year." He shook his head. "She wants him back, don't ask me why."

After a moment, Michael handed back the sketch. "Can't help you. Lots of soldiers around here look pretty much the same." He looked at him. "Kind of a miracle you recognized me, don't you think?"

"Miracles is what gets us by, son." Kennedy folded the likeness into his pocket wallet and put on his hat. "I thank you for your trouble."

With that, he headed toward the village center without looking back at the amputee. After a few moments, his men fell in step behind him.

The soldier knew something, no doubt about it. After his first glance at the sketch, something about the likeness had caught his attention. They would keep an eye on him. Douglas had been in the area, and it was a good possibility he was still there.

Michael watched them go. The man was lying, Michael had never seen him before, he was sure of it. He remembered every moment of his stay in that hospital ward in Washington, he had never fallen into fever, he slept so lightly that he snapped awake before anyone could approach his bed.

The one time he had lost consciousness he was waiting outside the field hospital on a litter and had awakened to find his left leg sawed off just below the knee. Near Strasburg, it was, in Shenandoah Valley. A pretty land it had been, before they marched through, torching the place, burning the fields, killing the livestock, even though most of the farmers were Mennonites, didn't hold slaves, wouldn't fight for either side. Sheridan told the men that there was no choice. They were at war. And the soldiers loved him, the wild Irishman, he fired them up, fighting alongside them. "Forward! Forward everything!" he had shouted, driving them onward.

Then Michael had been shot. He had heard the Minie balls whizzing past and had fallen into a crouch, keeping his head down. He hadn't even been afraid, it was a rout, the Rebs on the run. His leg was shot out from under him, and as he lay in the field, holding the bits together, he imagined in his delirium that it could still be salvaged. When he woke that night in the lantern-lit tent, he tried to sit up, then saw the bandage, and knew that at the age of twenty he was all but finished.

CHAPTER 32

AFTER ANYA LEFT HIS STORE, Brady busied himself with his customers. A stranger was leaning on the counter, absentmindedly tapping his foot. "I'll have one of those papers," he said, "if they're for sale."

"Sir, I'll be glad to take your money," said Brady.

After a moment, the man pulled a sheet from his jacket and slid it to Brady. "You seem to know everyone in the village. Ever seen this man?"

Brady looked at the sketch, then at the stranger. "Can't say that I have," he remarked. "Fellow actually looks a bit like you." He laughed, turning his attention to the fiddler, hooting with appreciation at a complicated run.

Kennedy tucked the newspaper under his arm and left the shop. At least he had learned what had happened to Blunt: he'd been murdered that very afternoon. Douglas would know that Blunt was not operating on his own. They would have to move very quickly. He might have already left the islands.

———⚬⚬⚬———

It was just after dawn, and Brady's shop was closed, the shades drawn. Douglas looked about to make sure he wasn't being followed then climbed over the sagging fence and went around to the back of the building. He rapped hard on the door, waited, then rapped again.

After a moment, the door opened a crack, and Brady gestured Douglas to come inside. "A man here looking for you here last night. Showed me a sketch."

"What did he look like?"

"Dark haired, older. From away."

Douglas nodded.

"Someone was with him, keeping watch by the door. Stocky. Sand-colored hair."

"What did you tell them?"

"Nothing. But a word to the wise, Mr. Douglas. You'd best be on your way as quickly as possible."

Douglas set his haversack on the table. "I need your help." He pulled out his pocketbook and placed it on the table. "It concerns Annie MacGregor."

Brady's eyes narrowed. "Now what business of yours would concern Mrs. MacGregor?" He shoved the wallet aside.

"I would like to leave something for her. In confidence."

"Why would it need to be confidential?"

He looked at the shopkeeper. There was no doubt that Brady cared about Annie, and for this reason, he knew that he could trust the man. "It is important that you get these things to her, but you must do it in such a way that there is no link between us. You must not connect her with me in any way. For her sake."

"For her sake." Brady folded his arms. "If you have put the lass in some sort of danger, I'll kill you myself."

"I'm leaving the islands, and I won't be back." He pulled from his satchel his books and the violin. "Do you have paper?"

Brady handed him a pencil, and he quickly filled the page. He removed from his packet a number of bills and folded them with the note into an envelope, handing it to the shopkeeper. "Tell her…when it's safe

I'll contact her through you. Wait a month then give her the money. When it can't be traced to me."

"I will do so." Brady pocketed the packet but when he spoke, his voice was still angry. "Have you wronged the lass, Mr. Douglas? Taken advantage?"

He was silent. Seamus Brady had put it all into terrible perspective. He had indeed wronged her, he had profoundly betrayed her. "You saw the men who are looking for me. If they think she is connected to me, they will harm her. Please take care of her," he said. "She considers you her friend."

"I am her friend. Good luck to you, then."

Douglas slipped down the alley onto a muddy lane that led to Riverside then walked to the dock, untied his boat, and rowed into the channel. To the east the sky was aglow, but upriver the islands were but shadows. He would pick up his gear at Maple then sail to the head of Wellesley Island and wait in one of the coves until night fell.

Then when the moon rose, he would row alone to Montreal. It was the only way to keep them safe, Annie and their child.

Anya awoke with a start, heart pounding. She had been caught in a nightmare, trying to make her way up the ladder from the hold of a ship. The vessel heaved and pitched and she could hear things sliding across the floor, one side to the other. As she came to herself, she realized that it was only a tree branch scratching against the roof of the inn.

As she lay in bed, she cradled her belly. She felt a bit of nausea, but that was a positive sign. Oh, how she wanted this child. In just a month or two they would be settled in their own home, in a cottage by the sea. She had studied the atlas at school with the children and remembered clusters of villages and islands along the ragged New England coast. Strange that she rued missing her last night in the little cabin, with the plash of the river, the call of the loons. She remembered her carpetbag under the cabin and hoped she could convince Jonathon to go back to retrieve it.

Ignoring the cracked mirror over the washstand, she splashed water on her face to revive herself, then looped her hair in a tight knot. Suddenly she was ravenously hungry and remembered the cheese and bread Brady had given her. It was already hot in the little room, so she gathered her things and left the inn, going down the servants' staircase so that she wouldn't have to see the clerk.

Making her way down to the river, she found a quiet place by the shore. Although it was early, the river was filled with boats; she could see a ferry plowing its way to Grindstone. How quickly life moved on. She hoped Erik had found his way home last evening. Surely his father would have come searching for the lad when he heard of the accident. They had already lost one son; it would be unbearable to lose another. She would not see them again, would never again hike the road past their farmhouse. She would miss the island, she realized. It had become her home.

After she finished eating her breakfast, she decided that she would stop by the train yard to say goodbye to Michael Burns. She owed him as much, she would not leave without saying goodbye.

As she approached the yard, she saw him standing in front of a freight car, a checklist in hand. He noticed Anya at once and came toward her.

"Is something wrong at the farm?"

"No, nothing serious, as far as I know. I was there yesterday."

He looked at her in silence.

"I didn't tell you the whole of it when you came by my cabin that time. Finn wasn't on the train. They told me he was in prison in Washington." Michael was so unresponsive that the rest came in a rush. "Seamus Brady sent a telegram and found out that Finn escaped. When you came by my cabin that morning…" He was looking at her so strangely that she couldn't finish.

One of the other workers was looking at them with interest and so Michael spoke again in a low voice. "Mrs. MacGregor, wait over there until I've finished checking these orders."

Anya watched uneasily as Michael looked inside the freight cars, counting shovels and barrels of tar. When he finally nodded his approval, a group of men began to load the wares onto wagons, and then he returned to her.

"Maddie and Charlie aren't doing so well on their own. Your da— Maddie said your father is trying to get the roof re-shingled." She stopped. She had no right to lecture him. "Well, I actually came to say goodbye. I'm leaving the island."

"Without waiting for your husband?"

"When I'm settled, I'll send my address to your father. I've already told Maddie and Charlie."

Michael began to look over his paperwork, his shoulders hunched in concentration. When he finally spoke, his voice was wintry. "I have information about your friend that may be of concern."

"What friend?"

"The one who spent the night in your cabin."

She looked at him. There was no point in denying what he knew to be true. After a moment she spoke. "What news?"

"Someone was here yesterday looking for him."

"What do you mean?"

"Someone from away. He showed me a likeness. Said the man was his sister's husband."

"What did you tell him?"

Michael began to shuffle through the papers on his table. "Nothing," he said finally. "I didn't say anything. "

She looked down, trying to compose herself.

"You didn't know he was married?"

"He's not. Neither am I." She turned and began to walk into town.

The lane was dusty from the wagons, and she ducked her head, moving aside to allow others to pass by.

"Anya!" Michael was hurrying after her, and so she stopped to wait for him.

"Anya." He gripped her arm. "The man was Southern. He tried to hide it, but I was down there long enough to know." He looked at her. "Do you have any idea what I'm talking about?"

She nodded. "Did he have red hair?"

"No," Michael said, surprised. "It was dark." Then he saw that someone had come upon them and was standing beside them, waiting patiently to get by on the narrow sidewalk. Michael pulled Anya onto the road and the man tipped his hat then moved on.

"However you have become involved, you must get out of it."

"I don't know what to do," she whispered, trying to contain her rising panic.

"Anya, go to the farm, you'll be safe there. I'll come home tonight, when I'm done with this."

"Michael, I'm leaving tonight, I won't be back. But I want you to know it's my brother I've been waiting for all these months. I never meant any harm with my lie. I'm sorry."

"Never mind about that," he said sharply. "Keep away from him, Anya. You don't know what they're after." He could see that she was set on her course, that he could not stop her. "They mean to find him," he said finally.

"We'll be far from here by morning. Don't worry." She reached up and hugged him. "Goodbye, Michael."

He watched as she hurried up the road, then he looked about. The streets were empty. He made his way back to the train yard, trying to control his uneasiness.

She went straight to the church and sat down in a pew near the door so that there was no chance that Jonathon would miss her. She was far too early, but she didn't know what else to do. She needed a place to think, to rest.

She measured the time by the chiming of the bells at the half then the full hour. At two o'clock, she stretched herself out to nap for a bit. She was so tired, not only from the sleepless nights but for the child she was carrying. The priest passed by her several times with a questioning look, and finally he spoke to her. "My dear, are you in need of confession?"

"No," she said. "Thank you, Father. I'm waiting for the evening Mass."

"You may wait here as long as you wish," he said kindly.

After awhile the church began to fill with parishioners. She looked around her, watching everyone who entered the building. No one paid any attention to her, crossing themselves with the holy water, moving to the front of the church, and genuflecting before sliding into their pews. The organ began to play, and in the candle-lit shadows she listened to words she had known from childhood.

Sanctus, Sanctus, Sanctus Dominus
Deus Sabaoth.
Pleni sunt caeli et terra gloria tua.
Hosanna in excelsis.
Benedictus qui venit in nomine Domini.
Hosanna in excelsis.

When she closed her eyes, she could almost imagine that she was back in the little stone church in Kilcar, her brother beside her, poking her in the ribs. Finn had been bored with church, but as a child she had loved the rituals, the incense and candles, the mystery of faith.

Then the priest turned and gave his blessing and Mass was over. The parishioners made their way up the aisles. The priest put out the candles and went into the refractory to remove his vestments.

The clock had already struck seven. Darkness would fall in less than an hour. The priest would lock the church in a few minutes; she couldn't wait any longer.

When the priest came down the aisle, she stood and said, "If a man comes looking for me, tell him I've gone home." She saw the look of distaste cross the young man's face. He thought she was using his church for an assignation. "My brother Jonathon," she added, then gathered her things and left.

On her way to the ferry, she stopped by Brady's Mercantile, but the place was locked, the shades drawn, the OPEN sign turned to CLOSED. Then she heard the ferry horn, the last one of the day. She grabbed her satchel and hurried to the landing.

CHAPTER 33

ANYA BARELY GLANCED AT THE PILOT as she paid her fare. She moved to the front of the boat where she would have the best view of the water. The islands were already shadows against the water and sky, but the river was still filled with vessels, so many that she could hardly keep track of them. There was no sign of Jonathon. Had he left without her? She knew he would do so only as a last resort. She thought about Michael's warning and found herself praying that Jonathon was well away from this place, away from harm. He would contact her when it was safe.

She wanted to weep with frustration as a stocky man hallooed from the pier, waving to the pilot to hold the ferry. He ran onto the boat shaking his head with consternation, laughing with the pilot about his rough night at O'Brien's Tavern. "My legs are heavy after a few pints of his ale," he said, shaking his head. He tipped his hat at the passengers. A few smiled in return.

If Jonathon had spotted someone he recognized in Clayton, he might have sailed upriver to Sackets Harbor, boarding a train to New York City where he could become all but invisible in the crowded streets. She closed her eyes and prayed.

Then she noticed the pilot looking at her curiously. "Don't worry, miss. Clear sailing all the way to Grindstone."

She nodded distractedly. Perhaps Jonathon was waiting for her at her cabin.

"Miss, were you on the ferry?"

Anya looked up. It was the jovial late-comer smiling down at her. She suddenly recognized him as the man who had been standing next to her and Michael on the lane into town.

He persisted. "During the accident?"

She shook her head and returned her gaze to the water, gripping her hands so that they would not shake.

When the ferry landed, Emmet Dodge was at the landing to meet them. Anya didn't know what to do. Was the sandy-haired man following her? But as she made her way off the ferry, he seemed to have lost interest in her, chatting with the pilot until all the passengers had disembarked. Relieved, Anya boarded the wagon.

Then he approached one of the draft horses and began to stroke its neck. "Beauties, these are."

"You comin' with us?" asked Emmet.

"Where you heading?"

"Down island as far as the schoolhouse." He nodded to Anya. "Evenin', Mrs. MacGregor. Your school made it through okay, but the big elm by the bridge went down." Then he picked up the reins and looked at the stranger. "You comin' aboard?"

The man shook his head. Anya watched him stroll down to the river, as if he had all the time in the world. The sun was setting and the river was cast with a rosy glow. A few skiffs dotted the water, but they looked like they belonged to fishermen of leisure. Did Jonathon live like this all the time, vigilant, suspicious? Would it always be this way?

As the wagon made its way down the island road, Anya was shocked by the damage caused by the storm. Here a barn stood, intact; there, just a few feet away, a house had lost its roof. Trees were shorn of their branches and crops were flattened in the field, a winter's worth of food all but ruined.

As Anya crossed the bridge, she weighed her options. She could wait for Jonathon, but his coming to the cabin had not been part of their plan. She would go to Maple under the cover of darkness. If he were still there, she would warn him, and they would leave immediately. She grabbed her carpetbag and headed down to river.

By the time Anya reached the shore, the sun had already set, but the afterglow cast enough light to see. Bats skimmed the water, and night-hawks fluttered amid the trees. She quickly bailed the canoe and tucked the shotgun under the thwart. She set her gear beneath the seat and shoving the boat into the water, climbed aboard. As she paddled toward Maple, the loons gave warning, their calls bouncing off the rocks, echo-ing throughout the islands.

———⊗⊗⊗———

He waited until he heard the farm wagon heading up the road then signaled to Kennedy and the others, who were waiting just off shore. When Kennedy got to the dock, he climbed into the skiff.

"She's on to me," he said. "Don't matter. The driver practically gave me her address. It's not far." He gestured in the direction the wagon was heading.

Kennedy nodded. "A few islands along the way. We'll check them first." He pulled away from shore, the other skiff following in his wake.

CHAPTER 34

DOUGLAS WATCHED THE SUN GO DOWN from his hide-out on Maple. His skiff was packed, set to go. He would not allow himself to think of her waiting for him in the church, of her growing realization that he would not come. He hoped that she trusted him enough to believe he was not abandoning her. Brady would eventually tell her, but until he did so, she might begin to doubt him. He had lied to her before.

The loons were calling to one another, their voices agitated. Something was troubling them. He listened more carefully. He heard a splash, then another. Someone was approaching the island. He climbed into the skiff and set his oars. The boat was light, fast, no one on the river could keep up with him. He would catch the current below Grennell and row all night.

At night the river was another world. Sounds traveled a great distance, and in the dark it was easy to lose one's bearings. With so little moon, she could barely differentiate between sky and river, but as her eyes became accustomed to the light, she slowly made her way through the shadow islands that marked the course to Maple.

She finally found the cut at Picton, and from there she spotted the outcropping of his island. As she got closer to shore, she could see his skiff. She would have missed it entirely had it not been for the white of the furled sail.

"Jonathon?" she whispered.

"Annie, why are you here?" His voice was low, sharp. "You must go back."

"They're here. Michael said they're showing your likeness in Clayton."

He knew then that he must take her with him; it was the only way to keep her safe. "Come ashore," he said. "Get into my skiff."

She paddled hard, and in a moment she had landed. She climbed out of the canoe, pulling her satchel from beneath the seat. He grabbed it from her and stowed it in the bow.

Then they heard the sound of oars hitting the water, boats moving swiftly toward the island. "Hide," he whispered.

She scrambled up the embankment towards the woods, and as she made her way in the darkness, she heard boats scraping on the rocks.

She realized that Jonathon was not behind her and stopped. Crouching down she looked toward the river, but it was so dark she could see nothing. Then someone lit a lantern. Jonathon stood on the beach. Three men circled him, their pistols trained at his heart.

"Who does this canoe belong to?"

"Me."

One of the men moved to the skiff and held up the lantern. "It's loaded with gear."

"Looks like you were on your way." Someone pulled out her carpet bag and dumped the contents on the ground. He kicked the stuff about. "Women's things. Find her."

"I'm alone."

The man lifted the lantern and the men turned toward the woods. "She's here."

Anya scrambled up the path, clawing at the branches, then someone was upon her, yanking her by the hair and dragging her down to the cove. He held the lantern to her face and in the lurid light, Anya saw that he was the man who had followed her to Grindstone.

"You don't need her, you have me now. Let her go."

"Jonathon!" Anya's voice was filled with despair. "I led them to you."

"No, ma'm. We spotted him same time as you did." Kennedy's voice had assumed the soft vowels of Mississippi.

"She's just an island girl. She doesn't know anything. Let her go."

No one spoke.

"I'll show you where I hid the money. If you harm her, you'll get nothing."

Kennedy spoke. "We won't hurt her. She's Irish, one of our own tribe." He looked at her. "Did he tell you he betrayed his own comrades? My brother was hanged because of him. Robbie was a war hero, but he was hanged no better than a horse thief." He turned to Douglas. "Why?"

Jonathon looked at him. He knew Kennedy, they had once shared a cause. "It was wrong."

"You could have kept your hands clean. You could have returned to Richmond."

"But I was already a part of it," Douglas said. "I would have been just as guilty."

"And you took the rest of the gold so we couldn't try again, couldn't even bribe the guards holding my brother in jail. Where is it?"

"I told you. In a munitions box, buried on the rise by my hut. I won't give it to you unless I know she is safe."

Anya spoke, her voice filled with fear. "Don't you see? The war is over."

"The war will never be over." Kennedy turned to the sandy-haired man. "Wait here with her. When you hear the signal, put her in the canoe, let her go."

Anya shrugged away from the man's grip. "Let us both go. Please. You'll have the money." She paused. "I'm with child. Don't leave our child fatherless."

Tom Kennedy looked at her for a moment. "Wait with her," he repeated. Then Kennedy said to Douglas, "Take us to the gold. Up to your cabin."

Jonathon turned to her. "Annie," he said. "*A rún.*"

"*A rún,*" she whispered, reaching for him.

Then Kennedy shoved him, pointing the gun at his neck. "Get going."

Two men followed behind, one of them lifting the lantern to light the narrow path.

As Jonathon made his way up the rise, he turned toward the shore, trying to catch sight of her, but the light was in his eyes and he was momentarily blinded. In a few moments they were at his hut, and one of the men threw open the door.

"Place ain't fit for an animal," he said.

Kennedy looked around with disgust. "Appropriate. Where did you bury the gold?"

"I won't tell you until I know the girl is on her way. You'll never find it on your own."

"She'll be safe," said Kennedy. "We aren't interested in her."

Jonathon knew this was not true. He had seen it in Kennedy's eyes when he learned that Anya was carrying his child. Her fate was sealed. It was time. He bent down, pulling the revolver from his boot.

Anya stood on the shore watching the lantern lighting the way to Jonathon's hut. The men's footsteps crackled through the woods, breaking twigs in the darkness. Someone stumbled, cursing, and the light jerked then righted itself. One of our own tribe, the leader had said. No, she was not one of them. Despite his promise, she believed that he intended to kill her. He hated Jonathon and this hatred extended to her, an eye for an eye, the Old Testament doctrine. And if he thought her pregnant, so much the better. He would end Jonathon's line.

When they found the gold, they would kill him. The gunshot would be the signal. Then the man standing next to her would shoot her. She would lay there on the shore, unburied, until someone discovered her body. A boat filled with fishermen, one of her students, Erik or Maddie. Anya saw it happening in a flash, as if in a dream. Here was where she would end her sorry life, in this forlorn place on the edge of the wilderness.

"*A rún*," he had said, my secret love. Anya hoped that he understood that she loved him, and that she would not let anything happen to their child.

The man guarding her shifted impatiently, looking at her, then in the direction of the light. She could no longer see it—they must have entered Jonathon's cabin. Was that where the gold was hidden? Or was it a lie, a diversion?

His grip on her arm relaxed as his attention focused on what the men were doing. Suddenly there was a shot, then a barrage of gunfire, cracking the night like firecrackers, the sound bouncing among the islands.

Anya slipped her hand into her pocket and pulled out her pistol then turned and shot him in the chest. One shot then the next. The man looked at her in surprise. As he crumpled to the ground, he raised his gun and pulled the trigger. She closed her eyes, feeling the bullet graze her leg on its trajectory into the bushes.

Anya dropped her empty gun, stepping away from him. Then she leaned over and picked up his pistol. Pointing it at him, she peered into his face. In the darkness she could not see much, but he was not moving and she was certain he must be dead. Anya instinctively made the sign of the cross, for him and for herself.

She shoved one of skiffs into the water then hauled herself aboard, groaning with pain. She heaved on the oars, standing with the effort, straining to be free of the gravel. The skiff broke loose and slid into the current and she headed upriver close to the shore.

Anya's breathing came in long gasps and she was aware only of the pain in her lungs and in her leg, a terrible burning. Then she stopped, listening. No one was following her. Blood coursed down her leg and so she pressed her petticoat against the wound, trying to staunch the flow. Then she tore a length free and wrapped it around her thigh, making a bandage. It soaked immediately. She took off her petticoat and wadded it against the wound, securing it in place with the soaked strip. She still had the man's gun. She would pull ashore at the head of Maple and make her way back to his cabin. She would find him and get him to Clayton, get him to a doctor.

Then she smelled smoke. The place had been torched. Soon the fire reached the crown of oaks, smoke roiling above them. The branches caught fire, popping and crackling and then it seemed as if the whole island were ablaze, a devil's torch lighting the night sky.

Anya felt herself growing faint and wondered if she was bleeding to death. She pressed hard with both hands on the bandage on her leg and started laughing, tears coursing down her cheeks. A terrible irony it was, both her brother and herself lost to a war that was not theirs to fight. Oh what a story to tell Finn when they met again in Kilcar. For there would be no heaven for them, only the green fields of their childhood, the green fields of Ireland. There they would spend their eternity.

She set the oars and closed her eyes, keeping vigil for Jonathon.

CHAPTER 35

ANYA WAS FOUND THE NEXT MORNING, adrift in the skiff, floating in the reeds near Picton Island. By daybreak, the river was filled with boats of all sorts. Some spoke of hearing shots in the night, but that was common enough by the waterfront, and at the time, no one paid any heed. It was the fire on Maple Island that had drawn the attention of the people of Clayton and the surrounding islands.

They did not connect the Irish schoolmistress to the incident on the island. A body had been found, the man shot to death. A hunter's camp had been burned to the ground, along with the trees around it, leaving a blackened scar on Maple visible from the mainland. No boats were found on the island, only an abandoned dugout canoe drifting in the shallows near Long Rock.

When Anya came to her senses, she explained to the constable that she had shot herself in the leg while practicing with her pistol, and that she had been rowing to Clayton for help when she had passed out from loss of blood. No one questioned her further about the matter, for she was only an islander and there was another murder to solve, one that involved someone from away.

Angus Burns took her back to his farm, where Maddie nursed her back to health in Cora's bed. Anya's memory of those days remained shrouded. Maddie told her that in her delirium she asked questions that made no sense, but she didn't tell Anya that she had called out for someone named Jonathon and wept for a baby she thought she had lost. Anya remembered that Charlie rocked by her bedside, humming tunelessly all the while, and that Maddie read newspapers aloud to cheer her. Most described the murder on Maple, linking it with all sorts of conspiracies. Anya's nightmares became mixed with the images, and she finally found words to ask Maddie to stop. Even in her illness, she realized that Maddie meant only to distract her.

One morning she awoke to find Michael standing at the foot of her bed, looking down at her. Stirring herself, she realized that she was finally able to sit up. "Michael, I need to get to Clayton. I am healed. Please take me today."

"You aren't well." He sounded almost angry.

"I need to see the body of the man they found on Maple."

"He was buried more than two weeks ago."

"Where?"

"Pauper's Field," he said finally. "In Clayton, down by the railroad tracks." When he saw her expression, he said, "When you are better, I'll take you to see the grave. There is no marking, just a plain wooden cross."

"I need to know who it was."

"Seamus Brady saw the body. He will be able to tell you what you need to know."

With that, she threw off the bedcovers and tried to stand. Pain shot through her leg and she felt herself grow faint.

Michael helped her back onto the bed. "I'll make you a pair of crutches. The doctor said that you will have the use of your leg, but you will need to start slowly, as I did."

"But I can walk. They didn't take my leg."

"You almost lost it, Anya." He looked at her. "When you are better I'll take you myself. But not until you have mended."

In the weeks that followed, Anya began to recover her strength. She walked farther every day, using one of the crutches Michael had made for her, finding strength in her anger and grief, finding strength for the sake of the baby. Oftentimes Charlie and Maddie accompanied her, Charlie mimicking her halting gait, the pup racing around in all directions, nipping at her crutch as if it were a game. She tolerated the foolish dog only because Charlie loved it so.

⸻⸻⸻

It was a fine, cruel September afternoon, the fields turned to gold, the sky a deep blue. Anya had made it all the way to the gate of the farm, alone for once, for the children had gone to the lower eight to help Michael and their father with the last stand of hay. She looked up as Emmet Dodge's wagon came slowly down the road. Riley began to bark and raced toward him. Calling her back was useless, so Anya walked toward them, hoping the dog would not follow Dodge all the way to the end of the island.

Then the wagon stopped, and Seamus Brady climbed down, stretching his arms. Both he and Emmet Dodge watched as she slowly approached.

" 'Afternoon, Mrs. MacGregor," Emmet said finally. "Good to see you up and about."

"Thank you, Mr. Dodge."

Brady turned to him. "Stop on your way back to the ferry. I'll be waiting right here."

Emmet Dodge looked from Brady to Anya, then nodded.

As the wagon pulled away, Brady shook his head. "I didn't believe a body could actually live out in this place. I'll feel it in my back tomorrow, after that ride."

"Seamus Brady!" She was all but overcome.

He folded his arms around her. "Mrs. MacGregor," he murmured. "What a time you've had. What a time."

She held him tight, then pulled away. "Seamus. I know you saw him. You must tell me what you know."

"I heard that you were gaining strength, Michael Burns stopped by to tell me. But I came to see for myself if you were sound. They told me you might have died."

"You can see that I am alive."

"Whose pup is this?" He leaned down to scratch its ears. He smiled. "This is your protector?"

"Seamus. Please. We need to talk. "

He nodded. "We will talk." He gestured toward the new-mown field. "Let's sit. I find the country most wearying." He shook his head. "Come back to town, Mrs. MacGregor. I told you before, this place is too rough for a lass such as yourself."

They settled in the meadow just beyond the lane. The pup ran off, following a scent. They watched it for awhile, then Seamus pulled her pistol from his pocket and set in on the ground in front of her.

"They found this on the shore of Maple Island." He waited for her to speak.

When she did not do so, he continued. "I was able to secure it before they investigated further."

"Seamus, I shot a man."

"You shot a man."

"I did. Twice. He meant to kill me, Seamus. I believe I may have killed him."

"Was it he who shot you in the leg?"

She nodded.

"Bloody shite."

He whistled for the dog, who came bounding toward them. Seamus scratched Riley behind the ears. "You got him first," he said mildly. "There's a good lass. You must have been practicing."

"I said a prayer. After I shot him."

"Did you then?" He made a vulgar noise. "Devil take the bastard."

She picked up the pistol and looked into the chambers. Then she put it in her pocket. "I guess I will be needing more bullets."

He looked at her, then laughed. "You are a wonderment."

"Seamus, why did you come all the way out here?"

"I told you, lass. I wanted to see with my own eyes that you were sound."

"I'm strong. I can walk with a crutch. I will always be a bit lame, the doctor says, but it doesn't matter to me."

He opened his coat and pulled out a folded purse. "Before he left, Jonathon Douglas stopped by the shop. He left some money for you. It's here."

She took the envelope from him, smoothing it, looking at Jonathon's unfamiliar script.

For Annie Mac Gregor

She traced the lines searching for something of him. Then she opened the envelope and read the letter. After a moment, she nodded then folded the note and replaced it in the packet.

"And these." He pulled from the sack the books and then the violin case.

With that she started to laugh. "A violin! But I don't play! She touched the case. "What will I do with it?"

Then she began to weep. "What will I do?"

Seamus let her be.

After awhile, she wiped her eyes. "Seamus, I must know the truth. Michael told me that you saw the body they found on Maple. Seamus. Do not allow me to wonder for my whole life if he is alive or dead. As I must wonder about Finn." She gripped his hand. "I can face the truth."

He looked at her, his expression guileless as a babe's.

"Seamus, the truth. You are my friend."

"You drive a hard bargain, Mrs. MacGregor," he said finally.

He was silent for moment, then patted her hand. "Lass, you already know in your heart."

She nodded. They sat together without speaking, until Emmet Dodge returned with the wagon.

E P I L O G U E

GRINDSTONE IS STILL A WILD PLACE, its trees so wind-blasted that they lean downriver, pointing the way to the sea. Even so, the tallest pines were taken years ago for ship masts, and when the Swedes came, the stonecutters, the island's very granite was carved away and shipped in the wake of the timber. Now much of Grindstone looks as mild as the farmland in Clayton, and the surrounding islands have become a summer playground for those from away.

The Thousand Islands, they are now called, a fanciful name that belies the islands' hard nature and history. Imagine, just ten years after the war ended, the Frontenac Hotel on Round Island has four hundred rooms, and ferries hurry to Clayton and back a dozen times a day, carrying patrons from Philadelphia and Baltimore. George Pullman, a wealthy railroad man, has built Castle Rest, with plans for a palace like one he'd seen on the Rhine. Americans, it seems, are intent on creating their own royalty after all.

To captivate the tourists, the newspapers create their own myths, and the island legends grow, of pirates and shipwrecks, unsolved murders. Maple Island stands most prominent in this regard. Touring boat operators cruise past the island, recounting tales of the ghost many claim to have seen, that of a tall, dark-haired man in a long coat standing on the shore, gazing intently upriver toward Grindstone. Writers have surmised that the ghost was one of Lincoln's assassins, a villainous ruffian from Mississippi named Lewis Payne. Some describe symbolic carvings on the body that was found, emblems of a secret Southern society, the

Knights of the Golden Round. One suggested that the victim's skull served as an ashtray in a barrister's office in the City of New York.

I cannot bear that his story be turned to fodder for entertainment, a hawker's tale. My mother told me that if the truth is not written, it will not stand, and so I have written something of what I understand of the man who called himself Jonathon Douglas. There are still missing pieces and ones that do not fit, and I can only hope that I have touched the heart of the matter.

I was twenty when I came to Grindstone, certain that my heart had become petrified by what I had learned of the world. Starved of light, starved of warmth was I that first winter, and in the thin twilight that presaged the long night ahead, I sometimes thought death my only salvation. My mother taught me that faith grows of necessity and there were moments when, had I not believed in the possibility that Finn would return, I might have followed her to the other side, walking toward the Atlantic on the frozen St. Lawrence until nature took its course.

A romantic would say that it was Jonathon Douglas who pulled me back to life, and I believe it to be the truth.

That fall, I re-opened the school on Grindstone, but when October arrived, I could no longer bear to stay alone in the cabin. Soon it would become obvious that I was with child, so I left my teaching position, and at Angus Burns's bidding, moved in with his family. There I made myself useful by tutoring Maddie and Charlie, sharing the books that Jonathon had given me. Neither Maddie nor Angus asked me about the father of my child, and for this I was grateful. Charlie delighted in my living there and in a small way my presence seemed to fill the gap left by his mother's death.

It was during that time that Michael became a true friend to me. When he understood that I was to bear a child, he offered to marry me. At that time I did not think Michael truly wanted to marry me nor did I believe I would make him a good wife. He was drawn to me, but it was the dark things in me that drew him, the very things that would hurt him the most.

I have come to believe that the sorrow we receive is fully matched with joy; it is the nature of things. In May, when my time came due, I gave birth to a daughter, our darling Katherine. It was Michael who made her cradle and who stayed up with me the night she almost died of pneumonia. As summer turned to fall, I saw that Michael had become part of the world again and that the love I had for him had grown deeper than sisterly. It was enough to build upon.

The next spring, after the snow had melted, Michael moved my father's coffin to the farm, all the way by barge from Kingston, Ontario. So Father has ended up in America, after all, in a peaceful spot under a chestnut tree, wild flowers all about, the river glinting gold on a summer's day. I talk to them often, my father and Cora. I hope she is pleased that I have married her son; I know she would dote on her grandchildren. Sometimes I sing songs for Aisling, sometimes I pray in a way that my mother would understand. I believe that in those moments, she is there among us, and Aisling as well.

Finn has not returned. Over the years I have heard nothing more from him. For too many families from the North and the South this has been the case. Yet I still believe that a letter could arrive any day. Meanwhile, I imagine Finn out west, trying his luck panning for gold or breaking the earth on his very own farm, a pretty wife by his side. A string of boyos following him to the barn, a dark-haired lass on his shoulder.

The farmhouse is noisy with our children, growing up sturdy and lively. We named our son Angus Thomas Burns but call him Finn for his merry laugh and his lanky stride. Our Cora Elizabeth came along two years later. Angus has aged before his time; he sits in front of the fire most days, even in summer, but takes pleasure in the hubbub around him. We have taught our children to respect the stories of his life's journey, of how he and Cora, factory workers from Glasgow, came to Grindstone, barely out of childhood themselves, and cleared the fields for the farm that now provides for us all.

Young Finn has learned the old tales, of Fionn MacCumhaill, his namesake, and spins a yarn almost as beguiling as Padraig's. Lizzie is a clever lass, and I have begun to teach her how to write, as my mother did me, my hand on her own as I help her to shape her letters. Kat is dark- eyed and lanky, as her father must have been as a boy, with a smile open to all the world. She has learned something of her father, whose violin she plays, a good man, a soldier for the other side in a war no one can truly fathom.

Charlie is growing into a fine young man, as quick-witted as his sister. He has taken a fancy to Jenny Robinson, and Angus has promised him some good land near the river. Unlike his brother, he will not have to go to war, and for that we are grateful. Maddie is more interested in learning than in farming and left Grindstone to attend the Normal School for Young Women in Watertown. She now lives in Clayton and teaches at the new school on Merrick Street, an imposing brick edifice far grander than the schoolhouse on the island. She is especially interested in history, and it troubles her that in so short a time, the war seems almost forgotten, at least in the North.

One fine summer day, I visited my old cabin, bringing Katherine along with me. The new schoolmaster was there, with his wife and child. I saw that a large addition had been built onto the place, and that trees had been cleared for a decent garden. We waved to the family as we passed by and walked down the path to the cove. Emil's old dugout had never been returned, and I wondered if he had come looking for it that fall. More likely he is making his way in a wilder place, the Laurentians or Georgian Bay. Perhaps he chose to stay with his wife and raise his own children and to quit his rambling ways.

We borrowed the skiff that was secured to a tree; it looked like the one in which I had made my escape, still sound, recently bailed. Katherine climbed aboard and I took off my boots and stockings and pulled it into the water. The river was calm, and it took no time at all to row to the island.

From the water, Maple looked smaller than I remembered. As we approached, I began to tremble, thinking of the night of the fire, so I stopped to compose myself. Rocking in the waves, I felt the sun on my face, and in a few moments, I was restored. When I opened my eyes, I saw my beautiful daughter looking at me quizzically, laughing. "Momma?" Then I saw that the scars from the fire were almost healed. In a few more years another crown of trees would shelter the place.

When we landed on the gravel shore, we climbed out of the skiff and pulled it ashore, and as I look up, he is coming down the path through the forest, his dark hair glinting in the sun. Smiling, holding out his hands to welcome us. And I understand at last my mother's belief that we are connected, forever, all of us and all living things, in some unknowable and sacred way.

Faith grows of necessity, for without it the world is indeed a dark and terrible place. One cannot make sense of it, the millions lost to famine, to war. How does one envision such numbers? An ocean of fish washed ashore, a sky-full of birds plummeting to earth. Michael still wakes at night in terror, and I hold him close, knowing he cannot rid himself of his visions any more than I can my own. We both have seen too much. Yet when I watch our children, Kat and Finn and Lizzie, racing up the lane to meet their da, I know that we have also been touched with grace.

Seamus Brady arranged to move Jonathon's remains to a proper cemetery in Clayton. There is no name on the stone, only these words,

SIOCHAIN ∞ SHALOM

Peace. And so by his unnamed grave I pray for Jonathon, that the spirit of the man who abides there has found his way home.

That night on Maple, when I thought for certain that I would die, I hoped that I would awake from this sad life and find myself in Ireland, with my mother and father and Aisling. And Finn as well, if his spirit were about. In Donegal, the fuchsia coming into bloom, the fields a green I have seen nowhere else in this world.

I no longer dwell on death as I used to, for in the passing years I have found much to live for. And I know that when I leave this earthly life, I won't return to Ireland. I will remain forever in this place, this rough and fertile land, so hard won.

THE END

ABOUT THE NOVEL

My husband's family ties to the St. Lawrence River date back to the War of 1812, and when our daughters were young, we spent summers in the Thousand Islands. A number of years ago, I wrote an adventure novel for my girls based on a favorite local legend, the ghost of Maple Island. The legend is described in John A. Haddock's *A Souvenir of the Thousand Islands of the St. Lawrence River*, published in 1895. The details are dramatic, of a handsome, genteel young Southerner hiding out on Maple Island in 1865. He was known to come into Clayton on a regular basis to purchase supplies and was often heard playing the violin at night. That fall, a fire was spotted on Maple Island, and the next morning, the young man's body was found. He had been murdered, his body mutilated with strange carvings. The murderers were assumed to be Southerners who had been spotted in the area, members of the Knights of the Golden Round. Haddock believed the victim to be Lewis (John) Payne, one of Lincoln's assassins; A. E. Keech theorized that it was Godfrey Hyams, who had been involved in the Confederate plot to bomb New York City. Some historians now suggest that the "Tragedy of Maple Island" may have been invented from the outset!

Who the mystery man on Maple Island actually was—or whether he even existed—is irrelevant to my novel. What interested me most about the legend was the role the Thousand Islands region played in the Civil War. The 94th Regiment Infantry fought in some of the most important battles of the war, Gettysburg, The Wilderness, Spotsylvania, and Cold Harbor; they witnessed the surrender of General Lee at Appomattox Court House. The St. Lawrence River was also strategically important to Confederate covert operations in Canada; during the war the islands were filled with spies and counterspies.

For years the legend of the mystery man intrigued me, and during my travels in Ireland, another character began to take shape in my imagination, that of a young woman from Donegal who settled on Grindstone in the aftermath of the famine years. Over a span of twenty five years, hundreds of thousands of Irish immigrated to Canada and the United States through Grosse Isle in Quebec, shaping the culture and events on both sides of the river. The novel grew out of the intersection in that seemingly isolated place of two major events of the time, the Civil War and the second wave of immigrants from Ireland and Europe.

Grindstone is a work of fiction, not history, and so I ask my readers to forgive the liberties I have taken to serve the needs of the plot, trusting that I have caught "the heart of the matter," as Anya tells us in the Epilogue. I thought it best, for example, not to trod on Grindstone family names! I have altered other facts; for example, I built a schoolhouse and brought the St. Lawrence skiff and railroad to Clayton a few years earlier than they actually arrived. While Anya, Michael, Jonathon, and Seamus are invented characters, John Headley, Godfrey Hyams, and the Kennedy brothers were actual participants in the Confederate operations to firebomb New York City. The newspaper articles, posters, and cartoon are authentic.

Sources of inspiration and enlightenment for *Grindstone* include *Fateful Lightning: The American Civil War*, by David Inglehart, William Hillenbrand, and Dennis Kennedy; *Confederate Operations in Canada and New York*, by John Headley; *1865: The Month that Saved America*, by Jay Winik; *Water, Wind and Sky*, by Ian Coristine; *A Pictorial History of the Thousand Islands of the St. Lawrence River*, editor, Adrian Ten Cate; *Grindstone: An Island World Remembered*, by Stanley Norcom; *The First Summer People: The Thousand Islands, 1650-1910*, by Susan Weston Smith; *Clayton*, by Verda S. Corbin and Shane Hutchinson; *Irish Folk Tales*, by Henry Glassi, *The New Oxford Book of Irish Verse*, Thomas Kinsella, editor; *A History of Ireland*, Mike Cronin; *The Great Hunger: Ireland 1845-1849*, Cecil Woodham-Smith.

ACKNOWLEDGMENTS

I have many people to thank for their help with *Grindstone*. David Inglehart, for his inspiration and faith in this project. A native of the Thousand Islands and producer of *Fateful Lightning*, he was an ever-present, enthusiastic resource without whom I would not have undertaken this work. My daughters, Caitlin and Dana, for their wisdom, clarity, and humor. And patience: since their teens, they have read a dozen iterations of *Grindstone*. Special thanks to Caitlin, who prepared the manuscript for publication. Nancy Meyers Lowe, Julia Flanders, and Mary Lynn Current, who patiently waded through the early drafts, nudging me in the right direction. Betty Stookey, who understood that *Grindstone* is ultimately about faith. My remarkable brothers, David, John Michael, Stephen Patrick, and Daniel Walsh. Mary Kennedy: "Just tell me what you need and I'll do it" (and she means it, always); Jeanne Mayell, whose passion for the novel inspired me to see it through. Ian Coristine, who provided generous and invaluable support, advice, and encouragement, as well as the stunning photograph for my cover. Dave O'Malley, who designed a cover that is both magical and unsettling. Marilyn and Alan Hutchinson, Corbin's River Heritage, for the contribution of the map of the islands. Dr. Charles Jellison, historian and writer, and Phyllis Gift Jellison, artist and muse: departed friends, I miss you every day.